Enter Frederick K. Bower

ANTHONY HOROWITZ

Enter Frederick K. Bower

DRAGON
Granada Publishing

Dragon Books
Granada Publishing Ltd
8 Grafton Street, London W1X 3LA

Published by Dragon Books 1985

First published by Arlington Book Ltd 1979
as *The Sinister Secret of Frederick K. Bower*

Copyright © Anthony Horowitz 1979

British Library Cataloguing in Publication Data

Horowitz, Anthony
    Enter Frederick K. Bower.
    I Title
    823'.914[J]   PZ7

    ISBN 0-583-30856-2

Printed and bound in Great Britain by
Collins, Glasgow

Set in Times

Contents

1

Frederick Kenneth Bower

Frederick Kenneth Bower was the most unpleasant boy in the world. In fact, he was more horrible than you could possibly believe. He was totally, completely and absolutely loathsome. There wasn't one single little thing about him that was even the least bit agreeable. But the worst thing of all was that, although he was only twelve years old, Frederick Kenneth Bower was the richest person in the world.

He lived in an enormous house in the most expensive part of Hampstead which is itself the most expensive part of London. This house had seventeen bedrooms, seventeen bathrooms, five dining-rooms, an indoor football pitch, a private cinema, an upstairs as well as a downstairs swimming pool and a solid gold escalator connecting the four floors. The garden was so big that several of the gardeners had disappeared without trace, swallowed up by the roses or, more probably, by the crocodiles which, along with many other exotic animals, inhabited the rockery. Next to the house there were seven garages, each one containing a different-coloured Rolls Royce with number-plates FKB 1 to FKB 7, one for each day of the week.

How did a boy come to possess such extraordinary wealth? The answer to that is that it was his father, Sir Montague Bower, who had built up the family fortunes and who, on his sudden and unexpected death, had left everything to his only child.

Sir Montague had been one of those peculiar men whose only pleasure in life is to have money: lots of it. His cigars had to be bigger than anyone else's, even though they made him feel quite sick. His wife had to have the most expensive mink coats, which she would wear, no matter how hot the weather. Every week the two of them would visit the Bank of England where they had a special vault, and they would count all their money, shrieking with laughter when they saw how much they had made.

Their business, by which they made these huge sums, was to build brand new office blocks and factories. They would look around London for suitable bits of land like parks, old shops and tumble-down cottages, and would somehow manage to buy them for a very low price. They would then build a sky-scraper or whatever, and would sell it for a huge profit. This was Sir Montague's business. It was called Bower Constructors.

Unfortunately, just when they were thinking of retiring and enjoying their wealth, a terrible thing happened, and you may well say that it really served them right. You see, although he had been constructing things all his life, Sir Montague had never cared very much for the safety of his buildings. To have done so would have cost a lot of money, and obviously the less you spend on something, the more you can hope to make when you sell it again.

In short, Sir Montague cut corners. Several of his buildings had gaping holes where the corners should have been. His own headquarters – a twenty-seven storey office block in the middle of London – had no foundations. Sir Montague had been too mean to pay for them.

And one day, as he was driving with Lady Penelope, his wife, to spend the day on his brand new yacht, it was this building that suddenly fell over and crushed them both. Luckily, although it hardly mattered to Sir Montague and Lady Penelope who were squashed so flat that at first the police mistook them for a carpet laid out in the street, the accident happened on a Sunday when the office was empty, so nobody else was hurt. But the result of it all was that only a week after his eleventh birthday, Frederick Bower found himself an orphan and the sole heir to the Bower millions.

Frederick, you will be shocked to hear, was not the slightest bit sorry about the fate of his parents. The sad truth is that Sir Montague and Lady Penelope had been so busy making money that they had hardly ever had time to see their only child. And when they did glance at Frederick, was was unusually plump and rather spotty, with awkward ginger hair and a tendency to whine, they were only too glad to hurry away again to their beautiful bank vault.

They had entrusted Frederick's upbringing to three nannies. Nanny Scrubb had been in charge of his personal hygiene and used to give him scorching hot baths every evening and clean clothes every morning. Nanny Swish had taught him to read and write, concentrating principally on bank statements and cheque books. And Nanny Sniff had made sure that he was healthy, feeding him great spoonfuls of cod liver oil and sending him straight off to bed if he so much as sneezed.

The first thing that Frederick did after his parents

had been buried (in a grave-yard so exclusive that you could only lie there if your name had been proposed and seconded by two other residents), was to sack the three nannies whom he had always hated. Indeed, out of sheer spite, he had them sent to a cold and dismal Old Nannies Home in the very north of Scotland where they were put to work knitting Post Office mail bags, and were fed only on porridge.

He then hired for himself an out-of-work chauffeur as he was obviously too young to drive. This chauffeur, who also became his personal valet and body-guard, was called Gervaise, and a more repulsive-looking man would be hard to imagine. He had only one ear. He was totally bald and had a huge scar running across the top of his skull. His nose had been broken in three different places (Hong Kong, Beirut and Marseilles) and he had massive, hairy muscles. He really did look like something out of a horror film.

However, Gervaise was very useful to Frederick. He would drive his young master to school in the morning, and would wait for him in the play-ground until the evening. Although a bully by nature, Frederick was very weak and was far too much of a coward to hurt anyone. So, if he felt like bullying any of the other school-children, he would say:

'Gervaise! I really don't like that boy Sington.'

And Gervaise would obediently lurch forward and bully Sington for him. Of course, all the other children disliked Frederick, but what with Gervaise protecting him, and the fact that he owned the school anyway, there was nothing they could do about it.

I could go on writing about Frederick Kenneth Bower until I had finished the book, but there is a story to be told. Still, one incident above all others shows just how unbelieveably awful Frederick really was, and how dangerous unlimited wealth combined with unlimited nastiness can be. I refer, of course, to the now famous Father Christmas Affair.

When he woke up on the first Christmas Day after his parents had departed from this world, Frederick was appalled to discover that Father Christmas had failed to visit him. His stocking – big enough to hold an elephant (which was indeed one of the things he was hoping to get) – hung from his four-poster bed, and for the first time in his whole life it was completely empty. Frederick was furious. He accused Gervaise of stealing his presents. He cried for an hour. He kicked his Siamese cat and cried for another hour when it bit him.

Then, after thinking things over for a while, he got into his Rolls Royce and ordered Gervaise to drive him to the nearest Television Studio, where they were half way through the All-Star Christmas Spectacular. Now, the TV studios had been built by Bower Constructors, and they still owed a lot of money. So when Frederick insisted on making a ten-minute broadcast, there was nothing the TV bosses could do to stop him.

So it was that all over the country, in the middle of the All-Star Christmas Spectacular, television screens were suddenly blacked out to reveal the ugly face of Frederick Kenneth Bower. And this is what he said:

'Ladies and Gentlemen. I am interrupting the All-Star Christmas Spectacular to tell you something very important, and what's more you'd better listen or I'll cancel the whole Christmas viewing and don't thing that I can't, so there!

11

'When I woke up this morning in my marvellously extravagant four-poster bed, I found that my stocking, what I put there the night before, was empty! There was nothing in it! Not a gold-plated sausage!

'Well, I've been thinking the matter over, and I've looked in a few books, and I've decided that obviously this Father Christmas character who is meant to fill up the stockings with everything I want – though I've already got everything I want and more, anyway – well, I believe that Father Christmas DOES NOT EXIST.

'I bet he's just a trick and it's really your parents who fill up the stockings and as my parents got squashed last year, there was nobody to fill up my stocking. And if I can't enjoy Father Christmas, I don't see why you should. So, let's get things straight. Father Christmas is a LIE. Santa Claus does NOT exist. It's all a MYTH.'

Can you imagine the results of this horrible broadcast? Families all over the country burst into tears. All the stars were far too upset to continue being spectacular. It quite ruined everyone's Christmas. But that was only the half of it.

When he heard about the broadcast, Father Christmas, who is as you know quite real and lives in a comfortable apartment flat near the North Pole, was absolutely furious. He actually wrote to the Prime Minister, threatening to give the whole of Great Britain a miss next year unless something was done.

Well, the Queen sent Father Christmas a telegram which read: 'We apologise most royally for this unfortunate error.' The Foreign Secretary took the first flight to the North Pole for serious talks on the subject with all Santa's helpers. No fewer than three committees were set up by Parliament to begin an immediate enquiry. It was a front page story in all the newspapers.

And the Archbishop of Canterbury wrote a letter to The Times, saying how sad he was that anyone could not believe in Father Christmas who was not only a fine fellow and an old friend of his, but also the person with whom he had shared a study at school.

2

The Secret Room

Frederick was bored.

It was a hot Wednesday afternoon in the middle of the summer holidays. Outside, all was silent but for the whirr of the crickets, the chirrup of the birds and the yells of the chef who had been hung from a tree by his thumbs for burning the toast at breakfast. The gardeners were clipping the lawn, keeping a careful eye open for crocodiles and the crocodiles were basking in the sun, keeping a hopeful eye open for gardeners.

When term had ended. Frederick had intended to go away for a month to his penthouse in New York, but had decided that he didn't like noisy cities. He had thought of flying in his private Concorde to the Bahamas, but had changed his mind because the weather there was so hot that he knew he would break out in spots. He had pondered over his castle in Spain, his palazzo in Venice, his hotel in Monte Carlo, his farm in Texas and his villa in Corsica. But coming to any decision was so difficult and the whole question was such a bother that in the end he had simply stayed at home.

Now he was sitting in his father's study on the tenth floor of the house, staring out of the window and wondering what to do next. So far he had carved his initials in the mahogany desk. He had spilt the ink and broken the pencils. He had telephoned a few numbers in Australia, upsetting the people at the other end of the line by waking them up in the middle of the night. He had taken the typewriter to pieces and failed to put it together again.

And he was bored.

Moodily, he got up and looked along the shelves. His father's shelves were filled with books, all of which looked far too dull to read (unlike this one, I hope). Titles included: *The Pleasures of the Pound* and *The Delights of the Dollar*. There was a twenty-four volume *Encyclopaedia of Investment* and even a *Pop-up Book of Gilt-Edged Securities*. Every single book seemed to be about money.

However, in the very centre of one of the longest shelves, his eye settled on a small, leather-bound book called simply *The Secret Room*. The three words were printed in gold on a white spine and there was no author's name.

'The Secret Room,' Frederick muttered to himself.

He reached out with a fat finger and thumb and tugged at the book. It wouldn't move. Frowning, he tried to wiggle it free, but still it remained stuck fast as if glued to the shelf. He pulled even harder, so hard in fact that he wondered why the book didn't rip in half. Finally, just as he was about to give up and go back downstairs, the tip of his finger came into contact with a button concealed behind the spine. He pressed it. There was a click. Frederick stepped back in amazement.

With a soft hum, the whole bookshelf was sliding into the wall, carried by hidden hydraulics. It slid for about six feet, revealing behind it – as the book has promised – the entrance to a secret chamber. Even as the shelf clicked into place, two neon lights flickered on and for the first time in his life, Frederick entered his father's inner sanctum, the place where Sir Montague had done his dirtiest work.

There was one desk, identical to the one which Frederick had been sitting at, except that this one was still cluttered with Sir Montague's things. There were two telephone books: a Yellow Pages and a Black Pages. A handful of pens and pencils were scattered amongst a sheaf of papers. These papers all concerned crooked deals of one sort or another but the writing was itself so crooked that Frederick couldn't read it. Otherwise, there was a paper-knife and a photograph of himself, the one unfortunately sticking into the other.

The room had no windows. A filing cabinet stood against the wall. It was labelled 'Blackmail Victims'. Frederick opened it. Inside the files were subdivided into Archbishops, Barristers, Chief Inspectors, Diplomats and so on all the way down the alphabet to a single, unhappy Zoologist. There were other filing cabinets for other areas of Sir Montague's business, but Frederick ignored them, moving instead to a plain wooden table at the far end of the room.

A pitch-black ebony box stood on the table. Even without opening it, Frederick could tell that it contained an unpleasant secret. Hand-carved scorpions scuttled across the lid and the key-hole was cut in the shape of a human-skull with a crossbones underneath. All that was lacking was the key.

Frederick, of course, loved secrets – and the nastier the better. So he went back to the desk and, taking the paper knife, slid it underneath the lid of the ebony

16

box and twisted. There was a dry crack as the wood broke. The box opened.

If Frederick was expecting a phial of poison or something like that, then he was disappointed, for the box contained nothing but seven sheets of paper. Three of these were letters, addressed to his father, and two were clippings from newspapers. The last two were an official-looking certificate and photograph.

Normally, musty old letters would not have interested Frederick, but because he was still sure that the box concealed some secret from his father's past, he read one of them. His eyes widened. He went over to the desk and read the letter again. Then the others. His mouth fell open.

An hour later, clutching the papers along with the Black Pages telephone book, he ran out of the room, almost tumbled down the golden escalator and rang the bell for Gervaise.

As Gervaise stamped into the hall (he had been enjoying a big piece of raw steak, which was his tea-time treat, so he wasn't happy about being disturbed), Frederick was already putting on his gloves and beaver-skin coat. He saw Gervaise come in and said, 'Get the car out, Gervaise,' and Gervaise replied 'Uuuuh!' which meant 'Yes, sir.' And two minutes later they were speeding through the northern suburbs on their way to the heart of London.

New Bower House, the new headquarters of Bower Constructors, was a magnificent building that stood, complete with foundations, near Trafalgar Square. It was thirty-nine stories high with great glass windows and steel girders. Fourteen fountains played in the

17

courtyard in front of it, and in front of them stood a marble statue of Frederick, sculptured by one of the world's most famous sculptors, showing him holding the world on a lollipop stick and about to eat it.

It was to the thirty-fifth floor of this building that Frederick, still clutching the documents, made his hurried way. The doorman saluted him. The receptionist quickly hid a woman's magazine she was reading and pretended to be busy. The lift-boy pressed the right button and winced when Gervaise stood on his toe. Within minutes of his entering, everyone in the building knew that Frederick had come to visit them.

Frederick was too young to handle the business himself, so he employed a manager to do this for him, and because the business was so complicated, the manager employed another manager to help. The two managers were called Toadwell and Cringer. When Frederick stormed into his office, Toadwell was waiting to greet him, while Cringer was polishing the desk.

Frederick's office was everything you would imagine an executive office to be. It was enormous and lavishly furnished with a luxurious, thick-pile carpet, only the most expensive cabinets and tables and a refrigerator filled with a range of executive drinks. One wall was completely taken up by windows, giving a wonderful view over Trafalgar Square, while the other was screened off by a set of silver Venetian blinds. A safe, about half the size of a London bus, stood mid-way between the two, joined to the wall by a thick electric cable.

'Good afternoon, Master Frederick,' Toadwell said when he saw his boss. 'May I say what a huge pleasure it is to see you. It's an enormous pleasure, isn't it, Cringer.'

'Oh yes, indeed,' Cringer agreed. 'I can't remember the last time I had such a massive pleasure.'

'Have you come to look at the accounts?' Toadwell asked.

'Everything is going very, very well, though I say it myself,' Cringer declared.

'Very, very, very well,' Toadwell added. 'In fact they couldn't be going better.'

'Would you like a glass of lemonade, Your Lordship?' Cringer enquired, hastily changing the subject.

'How about a nice piece of chocolate cake?' Toadwell suggested. He was so nervous that he had bitten his nails as far down as they would go and was now starting on his fingers.

Frederick, who was obviously in no mood for either lemonade or chocolate cake, sat down and scowled at the two men. 'Shut up, Cringer, and stop crawling,' he said. 'And don't bite your nails, Toadwell – or I'll get Gervaise to work you both over.'

Toadwell took his thumb from his mouth and shoved it into his pocket. 'I'm dreadfully sorry, Your Worship,' he said.

Cringer was sweating so much that a great drop of water trickled off his chin and landed with a plop on the carpet. 'Please don't set Gervaise on me,' he pleaded. 'He fractured both my knees last time.'

'I had four cracked ribs,' Toadwell said.

Both men looked on the verge of tears.

'All right. All right,' Frederick said. 'No one's going to hurt you. But I want action.'

'Action,' Toadwell said.

'Action,' Cringer cried.

'Stop repeating me, you dummies,' Frederick shouted. 'Is the computer plugged in?'

'Yes, Your Gloriousness,' Toadwell said.

'Right then. Give them the photograph, Gervaise.'

Gervaise took the photograph that Frederick had found in the ebony box and gave it to Toadwell. It showed a fair-haired boy, a little younger than Frederick.

'What a delightful boy,' Cringer muttered.

'How handsome he is,' Toadwell agreed. 'Is he a friend of yours?'

Frederick slammed his fist down on the table and leapt to his feet. 'No. He's not a friend of mine. I don't even know who he is, but I hate him. I loathe him. I despise him.'

The two men went pale.

'Actually,' Cringer stammered, 'he isn't that delightful at all now I think about it. No . . . not at all.'

'I meant he was ugly,' Toadwell explained. 'I didn't really mean he was handsome. No! I was being sarcastic.'

'Listen,' Frederick said, opening a cigarette box and popping a lollipop into his mouth. 'Can the computer tell me this boy's name and address just by looking at this photograph?'

'Of course it can!' Cringer said. 'New Bower House possesses the most advanced computer in the world. It's a tremendous computer with lots of flashing lights and whirly things . . .'

'. . . and it's connected to Interpol, to NASA, to the Kremlin . . .'

'. . . and it even talks!'

'It'll take just half a minute,' Toadwell promised.

'A few seconds,' Cringer concluded.

So, while Frederick sucked his lollipop and Gervaise leant against the wall, hoping he would be allowed to break a few more of the two managers' bones, Toadwell and Cringer drew up the Venetian blind to reveal a complicated machine, full of flashing lights, whirling tapes, keyboards and television screens.

'This machine can do anything,' Toadwell said as he punched a whole lot of buttons. The computer whined and blinked. Cringer pressed some more buttons. The computer whirred and rattled. Then Cringer fed the photograph that Frederick had given them into a sort of tray in one side, and pulled a lever.

Nothing happened.

Both men had gone green by now, as more than a minute had passed since they had promised Frederick the information that he wanted and Gervaise was already fitting on his knuckle-dusters.

'What's the matter?' Frederick demanded.

'Quite. What's the matter?' Toadwell said to Cringer.

'He asked you,' Cringer said.

'No he didn't!'

'Rotten computer,' Cringer moaned, drawing back his foot and giving the machine a kick.

'Ouch!' the computer exclaimed.

The kick seemed to have done the trick. The computer flashed its lights. The tapes went round and round. It whistled and yawned. Then it spoke.

'Herro,' it said.

'Herro?' Frederick repeated. 'What's that meant to mean?'

'It's a Japanese computer,' Toadwell explained.

'It was made in Japan,' Cringer added. 'It doesn't speak terribly good English.'

'Get out of here!' Frederick snapped.

'Geh rara hah!' the computer repeated.

Both men started bowing as they tried to leave the room backwards, but they collided with each other and fell over in a heap on the carpet.

'One moment!' Frederick ordered. 'I have some extremely important papers with me and I want to put them somewhere safe. Where do you suggest?'

'The Bank of England,' Toadwell said, as he picked himself up.

'No. They must be near me – where I can be sure they're safe.'

'How about the safe in your own office?' Cringer asked.

'That's a good idea,' Frederick said. He was cross that he hadn't thought of it himself. 'But is it safe?'

'It's a very safe safe,' Toadwell replied.

'It's made of solid steel. Two yards thick,' Cringer added.

'A tank couldn't burst it.'

'An atom bomb couldn't dent it.'

'Then how do I open it?' Frederick asked.

Toadwell smiled. 'It's easy, O Great One,' he said. 'The safe is connected to the computer. All you have to do is enter the password – a word known only to your glorious self – and the safe will open automatically.'

'But suppose I forget the password?'

'Just key in the name of the thing you love most in the world,' Cringer suggested. 'That way you'll never forget.'

22

'All right. Get out,' Frederick said. He wanted to get down to business.

'God bless you,' Toadwell sighed.

'I worship the carpet beneath your feet,' Cringer said.

And both men left in a hurry, glad to get away from the frightful Frederick and the gruesome Gervaise.

As soon as they had gone, Frederick turned to the computer.

'What's the boy's name?' he demanded.

'Boy in photo is named Lobin West,' the computer said.

'You mean Robin West?' Frederick snarled.

'Yes. Lobin West.'

'And where does he live?'

'Address is 64 Windsor Gardens, Pinner. Pinner is small town in Rundon.'

'Where's Rundon?' Frederick asked.

'Rundon is capital of Ingrand.'

Frederick drew a doodle on his blotting pad and popped another lollipop into his mouth. 'I want this West character dead,' he said. 'I want him mashed up, made into mince mortals, broken into little bits. I must be rid of him.'

Gervaise smiled, showing a line of broken teeth. The computer hummed and whirred.

'But we've got to be careful. We can't risk anything. If people find out about my connection with the brat, it could mean trouble.'

Gervaise frowned as he tried to work out what 'connection' meant. He had difficulty with long words.

'So I think I'll send him a box of chocolates from my

own store,' Frederick continued. 'How much rat poison is there left?'

'Lat poison!' the computer muttered.

'Rat poison?' Gervaise asked.

'The poison made by my rats, you dum-dums,' Frederick explained impatiently. 'We'll need lots of it. A gallon. I want you to put a big dollop of poison in all the tastiest, most mouth-watering chocolates. And then we'll send them to Robin West and he'll just sniff one of them and that will be enough to finish him for good and hooray for that.'

'Hooray,' Gervaise said.

'Hoolay!' the computer sang.

'There is one thing though,' Frederick added. 'Supposing he doesn't like chocolates? Supposing he gives them away? What if they get lost in the post so that he never even receives them?'

'Uuurk?' Frederick asked.

'I think I'd better be absolutely sure that this boy does come to a fast and horrible end.'

Frederick finished the doodle on his blotting pad. It was a picture of a bomb. Then he opened the Black Pages telephone book that he had found in his father's study and ran a finger down the index, stopping midway through the M's. He picked up his private telephone and dialled the number he had found.

'Hello?' he said when he was connected. 'Is that Murder for Money & Company? I want to speak to Spider and Moss Kito.'

3

Robin West

Meanwhile in Pinner, Robin West was just finishing his paper-round. Robin is, as you may have guessed, the hero of this book. But just in case you're thinking that Robin is one of those clean-cut, unbelievably good children, the sort who have a nasty habit of appearing as heroes in books, you'll probably be glad to hear that this is not the case. It's true to say that compared to Frederick, he was a saint. But like most twelve-year-olds, he certainly wasn't popular with everybody.

He was extremely unpopular with Mr Sylvester, the owner of the newspaper and grocery shop. He greeted Robin with a scowl.

'Good evening, young man,' he said.

'Hello, Mr Sylvester,' Robin replied.

'I see you've finished your evening paper-round,' Mr Sylvester sneered.

'Yes, Mr Sylvester.'

'But those were the morning papers you were delivering.'

'I overslept,' Robin explained.

'By ten hours?' Mr Sylvester cried. 'Those papers should have been in the letter-boxes at eight o'clock this morning!'

'I'm sorry,' Robin said.

'Sorry? Sorry! Is that all you can say? Well . . . that's not all. I've had a lot of complaints from my customers. Mrs Higgins got the *Financial Times* instead of the *Mirror*. the vicar got the *News of the World*, and his wife was not amused to find naked women all over her doorstep. While Mr Beer, the pub-owner, got the *Church Gazette*. What do you have to say for yourself?'

'I was in a hurry,' Robin stammered.

'Well, you can jolly well hurry away from my shop,' Mr Sylvester screamed. 'You're sacked. You're fired. I've never had a worse paper-boy in thirty years. A trained monkey could deliver the papers better than you. Get out!'

'What about my money?' Robin asked. He wasn't afraid of Mr Sylvester.

'Your money?' Mr Sylvester was crimson with rage, his small moustache quivering like a caterpillar. 'I've a good mind to take a belt to your backside. In fact, I think I'll do just that.'

With a sniffle of anger, Mr Sylvester undid the black leather belt which he wore around his waist and would have grabbed Robin had not his trousers immediately fallen down. Instead, as he took a step forward, he tripped up and fell over into the deep freeze which clanged shut on top of him. Robin quickly leaned on the lid, and fell about laughing while Mr Sylvester screamed.

A moment later, he was off down the street as Mrs Sylvester, alerted by her husband's cries, rushed into the shop, brandishing a broom. By the time she had let him out, Robin was two blocks away.

When he got home, the first thing he did was to tell his sister, Mary, what had happened. The two shared all their secrets and never argued like most brothers and sisters, but although Mary was only a year younger than Robin, you could not imagine two people less like each other. Robin had straw-coloured hair and bright blue eyes and was already quite tall for his age. Mary had black hair and dark brown eyes and was several inches shorter than her brother.

In fact, they weren't really brother and sister at all. Robin had never known his real parents, for he had been abandoned in St Mary's Hospital, Paddington, a few days after he was born. Mrs West, although she was quite able to have children of her own, had fallen in love with the little bundle and, once all the right forms were filled in, had adopted the boy as her own.

Mrs West was a delightful woman. Everyone in Pinner knew her and liked her. Unfortunately, however, she had one major failing which was that she was rather eccentric and always forgot everything. She would walk into a shoe-shop and ask for a loaf of bread because she had forgotten to read the name on the door. Whenever she parked her car, you could be sure that she would be unable to find it again. Once she had even gone shopping in her pyjamas because she had forgotten to get dressed before going out.

The result of all this was a sad one. Her husband, Edward West, who was a bank clerk, had gradually become more and more exasperated with his absent-minded wife. And one day, when he opened his lunchbox at the bank and found, instead of ham and tomato sandwiches, a whole lot of wool and knitting needles (and even at that moment, Mrs West was trying to knit a jumper with two pieces of bread and a slice of ham), he had decided to leave her and live by himself. Edward West was a kindly man, but he was also extremely tidy and methodical. And so it was that he left Mrs West and later married a librarian who kept all his things in alphabetical order and never forgot anything.

Mrs West had brought up Robin and Mary in their semi-detached house in Pinner. They were not very rich, as Mrs West was quite unable to stay in one job for very long, and although she did try to be a strict mother, she wasn't even suited to this task, as she now proved.

'Robin,' she said, when she got back into the house that evening. 'You've been very bad.'

'Have I, Mother?' Robin asked, his eyes wide open in innocence.

'You know very well that you have,' Mrs West continued. 'I've just been told about it by that poor Mr Spencer . . . or was it Mr Wilson? Oh dear! Who was it who was complaining about you?'

'Mr Sylvester?' Mary suggested.

'That was him! Really, Robin, you were very bad to. . . to . . . Oh heavens! I've quite forgotten what you're meant to have done.'

So Robin, who was always honest with his long-suffering mother, recounted what had happened. At first she frowned at him in an adult manner. As he went on, her lips began to quiver. And when he described how Mr Sylvester had fallen into the deep freeze, she burst into uncontrollable laughter. By this time, of course, she had forgotten that she was meant to be cross, and all three went into the kitchen for tea. They almost had to eat peaches on toast, followed by sardines and custard, for Mrs West had got the tins the wrong way round, but fortunately Mary managed to sort things out for her muddled mother.

After supper, when they had done the washing up, they turned on their black and white television for an hour before bed. The set was permanently tuned to ITV, as the other channels had never worked since Mrs West had watered the television, confusing it with a cactus.

As the screen flickered to life, the news ended and an advertisement began. It was an advertisement for chocolates with a young man diving off a cliff and swimming across a shark-infested lake . . . and all because his lady loved that particular brand. When she saw this, Mrs West leapt to her feet and clapped her hands together.

'Sharks!' she exclaimed.

'Where?' Mary cried.

'No . . . I don't mean sharks. I mean chocolates!' Mrs West thought for a moment. 'Robin, I quite forgot! Go and look in the kitchen cupboard. Quick!'

Robin did as his mother told him, and a moment later came back in, carrying a heavy box of expensive and very delicious chocolates. Written on the red velvet lid was the name, 'Bowers Chocolate Selection. Thirty luxurious fillings in the very finest dark chocolate.'

'What is this?' Robin asked in amazement. 'Mother, how could you afford anything like this?'

'I didn't buy them,' Mrs West replied. 'They came in the post this morning for you. I opened the parcel by accident. Look – there's a letter that came with them.'

And rummaging in her handbag, she pulled out a letter.

'To Mr Robin West of Pinner (it read),

Kongratulashuns! You have wun first prise in our

29

kompetition. We inclose a delishous box of our best chocolates which we hope you will enjoy.

Signed: the manajers of Fortnum & Bower Department Store, Piccadilly.

PS: make shore you eat a lot of them!'

'Golly!' Mary exclaimed, her mouth watering.

'It's very odd, I must say,' Robin said.

'What's so odd,' Mary asked, reaching for the biggest of them.

'No. Wait a minute.' Robin stopped her. 'How can I have won a competition at the Fortum & Bower Department Store when I haven't even been in it?'

'Does it matter?' Mary said.

'Do you think it might be a mistake?' Mrs West asked.

'I don't see how I can have won them,' Robin said. 'And besides, there's something rather fishy about this letter. It's full of spelling mistakes.'

'I thought that was a bit peculiar too,' Mary agreed.

Robin looked at the chocolates again, and immediately his fears melted away. They were spectacular chocolates. The list on the lid of the box included such delights as 'Italian strawberry whirl' and 'Brazil nut cluster' and 'Super-cream toffee whip.' After a minute he couldn't resist them any longer.'

'If they've been sent to me, I don't suppose there's any harm . . .' he said, as he stretched out his hand to take one.

But now Mrs West stopped him. She was by nature a nervous woman because her absent-mindedness was always getting her into trouble, so she wanted to be sure that they were doing the right thing.

'No, Robin,' she said. 'Let's not touch them. It may

30

well be a mistake, and we wouldn't want to deprive someone else of the prize.'

'But mother . . .' Mary began.

'No. We'll put them on a shelf tonight and ring Fortnum & Bower in the morning. Then, if everything's all right, we can eat them without feeling uncomfortable about it.'

Well there was a bit more arguing, but in the end Robin and Mary had to agree with their mother. After all, twelve hours isn't long to wait, especially when you're asleep. So they kissed their mother, cleaned their teeth and went to bed.

One hour later, after News at Ten, Mrs West followed them upstairs and, having cleaned her teeth with a nail-brush and washed her hands with a bar of chocolate, she too fell into a sound sleep.

At three o'clock that night, a most unusual thing happened. A pane of glass in the window of the dark and empty kitchen suddenly fell out with a quiet tinkle and a gloved hand was shoved through the hole to release the latch. A moment later, a man wearing a dark pullover, dark trousers, a dark hat and carrying a dark sack, climbed quietly into the room.

This man was called Sam Fingers and he was a professional cat burglar. In fact cats were only one of the things he stole. He also stole candlesticks, video tape recorders, jewellery, fur coats . . . anything he could get his hands on. And while the Wests slept upstairs, he went about his business, opening cupboards and pulling out drawers.

Sam was certainly disappointed with the Wests' home, which was far poorer than most of the houses on his beat. It didn't even have a colour television. But he still managed to fill his sack with a few bits and pieces and was about to leave the same way he had broken in when he saw the chocolates which Mrs West had placed on the kitchen shelf.

Sam didn't really like chocolates, but being greedy (like most thieves), he pulled one out with his gloved hands and swallowed it – without even looking to see if it was a nutty one or a soft centre. Then he picked up the rest of the box and was about to hide it away in the sack as a present for his wife – when she got out of prison – when he suddenly felt rather ill. He was giddy. He broke out in a sweat. His stomach hurt.

Sam Fingers gave one last great belch and then without another sound fell over dead in the middle of the carpet.

4

The Second Attempt

A week after the excitement had died down and the police, the newspaper reporters and the neighbours had gone back home, Robin and Mary were sitting on a bench in the local park, feeding the pigeons. Unlike most of their friends, they had been unable to afford a holiday abroad, and so relied on each other for company.

They still had no idea where the chocolates had come from. The department store, of course, had sworn that it was in no way involved. But both of them knew that they had had a very close escape and but for the unfortunate Mr Fingers they might well have eaten the chocolates themselves.

The most worrying aspect of the whole affair still hadn't occurred to Robin, nor to the police, nor to Mrs West. It had, however, occurred to Mary.

'Robin,' she was saying. 'Why should anyone want to kill you?'

'Kill me?' Robin gasped. 'What do you mean, Mary?'

'Well, those chocolates were addressed to you.'

'It must have been a mistake. That's what the police said. I mean, why should anyone want to kill *me?*'

'That's just what I asked,' Mary said. 'Whether you like it or not, it was your name on the parcel and your address.'

'You're just trying to frighten me,' Robin said. 'I can't think of anything more ridiculous.'

'I hope you're right,' Mary said.

Now, had they looked up at that moment, they would have had every cause to be frightened. For, as they fed the birds, a gleaming silver Mercedes drove past on the road behind them. And if they had chanced to see the two men inside it, they would have got on the first train to China. And if they had known that these two men were called Spider and Moss Kito who that they were the two top killers of 'Murder for Money & Company' and that they were carrying a photograph of Robin West, they probably wouldn't have come back again.

Spider was a short, fat man with a great mop of black curly hair and ridiculously thin, hairy arms and legs. His eyes bulged out of the side of his face and his mouth was twisted into a wicked grin. Moss Kito, who was driving, was exceptionally tall and lean. His silver hair stuck out like strands of barbed wire. He was a good deal older than Spider and was grey all over but for his two front teeth which hung over his lower lip, gleaming white and sharpened like pins.

'Moss,' Spider was saying.

'Yes, Spider?' returned Moss.

'Whassis boy called?'

'Robin West,' Moss told him.

'He's only twelve years old,' Spider muttered.

'So what?'

'Well, I was just wondering if . . .'

'Is your conscience bothering you, you blithering idiot?' hissed Moss.

'Well, Moss. It would be like my own son.'

34

'And what happened to your son, Spider? He fell down a lift-shaft.'

'That was an accident, Moss. I was playing with him.'

'Well, now you can play with Master West, Spider. Geddit?'

'Yes, Moss,' Spider replied. 'You're the boss, Moss.'

They drove on in silence. After a while, Spider took a package out of the glove compartment.

'What are you doing, Spider?' Moss asked.

'I'm getting the bomb ready, Moss,' Spider said.

'You cretinous clot!' snapped Moss. 'You incapable nincompoop! What do you mean by getting the bomb ready in the car?'

'I . . . I . . .' Spider began.

'And what if I decide, just for a bit of fun, to knock over a policeman or two? The smallest jolt could blow us both sky high. Honestly, I don't know why I work with such a ludicrous lout.'

'Sorry, Moss. I didn't mean to make you cross, boss,' Spider muttered, hastily putting the package away.

A few moments later, the car pulled up beside the pavement and the two men got out and walked into the nearest shop, which was none other than Mr Sylvester's newsagent and grocery. Moss had already made some enquiries about Robin's activities and had been told about the newspaper round. It was his plan to slip the deadly package containing the bomb into Robin's delivery sack, and he was now in the process of spying out the land.

When the two assassins entered the shop, Mr Sylvester was busy sticking new price labels on his tins and

35

stealing the special offers out of the cereal packets. When he saw the strange figures of Spider and Moss, he almost fell into the deep freeze again. Never in all his life had he seen two such sinister people. One tall and thin, the other short and fat, they stood dressed in black, like ghosts from his worst nightmares.

'Can I help you . . . gentlemen?' he quivered.

'I wish to buy some fish-fingers,' Moss said, as politely as he could.

'I didn't know fish had fingers,' Spider whispered.

'Be quiet, you clown,' Moss hissed, kicking his accomplice in the shin.

Mr Sylvester wrapped up a box of fish-fingers and gave it to Moss. As their hands touched, he noticed that the stranger had hands of ice. He couldn't help shuddering.

'Incidentally,' Moss continued as he paid for the purchase, 'Will that charming delivery boy of yours be in to collect the papers tomorrow morning?'

'Charming boy?' Mr Sylvester repeated. 'You don't mean Robin West, do you?'

'The very same. Such a delightful fellow,' Moss said.

'Bless his little bones,' Spider added.

'If you gentlemen are looking for Robin West, you won't find him here.' Mr Sylvester became quite carried away. 'He's a little monster. All that business with the poisoned burglar. I bet he had a hand in it. I've never met . . .'

'Does he still work here?' interrupted Moss.

'No,' the grocer replied. 'I sacked him last week, and not a moment too soon.'

Moss received this information quite coldly, although he knew that he would have to change his plans. He gave Mr Sylvester a polite smile – at least, that's what he would have called the crack that appeared in the bottom of his face, although most people would have found it rather horrible.

'Please don't tell little Robin that we asked after him,' he said. 'You see, I'm his Uncle Sidney from Florence.'

'And I'm his Uncle Florence from Sydney,' Spider said, adding 'Aaargh!' as Moss stamped on his foot.

'Yes,' Moss continued. 'I've got a little present for sweet young Robin, but I want to surprise him. He mustn't know I'm here or it will spoil it for him.'

'Well, all I can say is that Robin West is a nasty little boy,' was all Mr Sylvester could say. 'And furthermore, if I were you two gentlemen, I wouldn't give him anything except for a good hiding. Let me tell you . . .'

But before Mr Sylvester could finish his sentence, the two unusual men had turned their backs on him and walked out of the shop, leaving the fish-fingers behind.

Now Mr Sylvester was one of those men who like to have the last word. So when, in his lunch-hour, he happened to come across Robin and Mary, who were still in the park, he couldn't resist marching up to them with a superior smirk on his face.

'Master West!' he cried as he approached.

'Hello,' Robin said, politely.

'Don't you hello me, you young puppy,' Mr Sylvester said, quite unreasonably. 'I've just met your Uncle Florence and your Uncle Sidney who have come on a surprise visit.'

'Uncle . . . ?' Mary began.

'You be quiet when an adult is talking,' Mr Sylvester shouted. 'They said they had a present for you, but I told them what a nasty character you were, and I hope they change their minds. Boys like you don't deserve presents. You deserve a good caning. I was caned twice a day for a whole year when I was at school and it didn't do me any harm. Oh no! In fact I enjoyed it!'

And with an insane laugh, Mr Sylvester strode off back to his shop.

Mary and Robin were quite astounded. For a start, they both knew perfectly well that they didn't have either an Uncle Sidney or an Uncle Florence.

'What on earth do you think he's on about?' Robin asked.

'I don't know,' Mary replied.

'I don't like the sound of it at all,' Robin said.

'You don't think . . .' Mary didn't finish the sentence. She and Robin had been badly scared by the chocolate incident and though they hadn't really talked about it, they both feared that Robin's mysterious enemy might strike again. Worse still, the police were so certain that the poison had been meant for someone else that they hadn't offered Robin any protection – which they would have done if he'd been a film-star or a politician or even someone just a little bit famous.

They sat in silence for a minute. Then Robin said, 'Listen, Mary. I think we ought to get back home at once.'

'I agree,' Mary said.

'But we'll go back separately.'

'Why?' Mary asked.

'Well, it seems that it's me they're after. After all, the chocolates were sent to me. Maybe these two

38

strange men don't mean any harm, but if they do, it would be better if you weren't with me to get hurt too. And besides, if necessary, I can run faster than you.'

Mary wanted to stay with her brother, but she couldn't argue with such good sense. So they agreed that they would walk home by different routes and would pretend that everything was normal so as not to alarm the two strangers. And when they got home, they would tell their mother who would call for the police.

Robin went home the long way, over some wasteland and through a maze of back-streets, and he was neither seen nor stopped. Mary, however, went right through the centre of Pinner. This was a mistake.

Just as she reached the point on the main road where Windsor Gardens turned off, and just as she was thinking that perhaps there had been nothing to worry about after all, a great hairy hand suddenly grabbed her by the neck, quite taking her breath away. And when she turned round, she found herself looking into the swollen eyes of the murderous Spider.

'Excuse me, young lady,' Spider said. 'Me and my boss, that is, er, my good friend . . .' he pointed to a shadowy figure sitting in a Mercedes across the road '. . . we was wondering if you could do us a favour.'

'Y . . . y . . . yes?' Mary stammered.

Spider produced a brightly wrapped package. It made a loud ticking noise.

'Would I be right in thinking that your brother is none other than that little darling, Robin West?'

'Y . . . y . . . yes,' Mary stammered again, more frightened than ever.

'Well, he bought this here present as a gift for your

39

dear mum. You wouldn't by any chance be seeing him in the next . . .' he looked at his watch '. . . four and a half minutes?'

'I'm just going to have lunch with him at home,' Mary said, hardly able to breathe.

'Then could you be so kind as to give him this bomb, which I have wrapped up for him?'

'A . . . bomb?' Mary cried.

'No! No! Did I say that?' Spider shook his head, rotating his eyes. 'It's a clock. But it cost him a bomb! That's what I meant. Will you give it to him?'

'Yes,' Mary sqeaked.

'And that's for you.' Spider gave her ten pence. 'You can buy yourself some sweeties, sweety. But do make sure you give him the clock first.'

And with that, Spider scuttled across the road as fast as his legs would carry him.

Mary ducked round the corner, stopped and put the parcel up to her ear. It was ticking very loudly. Now Mary was no fool, and had been brought up with one strict rule: never accept parcels from strangers.

She didn't like to think what was in the parcel. But her deepest feelings told her to get rid of it. Yet what could she do? Robin had never mentioned buying a clock – but suppose he had, as a surprise? He would be furious if she threw it away just because she was frightened. But on the other hand, supposing the two men in the Mercedes were the two men Mr Sylvester had seen, and supposing they were up to no good . . . ?

It seemed that she had been holding the parcel for hours, although less than a minute had passed. Now she made up her mind. She shouldn't have taken the parcel from a stranger, so the best thing would be to give it back.

The traffic along the main road had come to a standstill at the red lights so, with her head well down, Mary was able to cross over the road keeping in between the cars so that the two men in the Mercedes couldn't see her. The Mercedes showed no sign of moving off.

Then, one step at a time, and as quietly as she could, she crept up to the Mercedes and opened its boot a fraction of an inch. Fortunately, it was unlocked. Then she slid the parcel into the car's boot, closed it again and quickly crossed to the other side of the road.

Inside the car, Moss was counting the seconds on his watch. 'You're sure the brat will give it to her brother?' he asked.

'Yes, boss,' Spider replied.

'Excellent,' Moss whispered. 'Then in thirty seconds, the whole West family will be blown to pieces. What a brilliant plan! No wonder I'm the highest paid man in Murder for Money & Company.'

'You're terrific, Moss,' Spider agreed.

'Countdown starting NOW!' Moss cried. '20 . . . 19 . . . 18 . . .'

'Excuse me, Moss,' Spider suddenly said, creasing his brow.

'17 . . . 16 . . . 15 . . .' Moss continued.

'Moss!'

'Yes?'

'Do you hear a funny sound in the boot?'

'What sort of funny sound?'

Spider's face had gone green. 'A sort of . . . ticking sound?'

41

'What?' Moss hissed in his loudest whisper.

'There's a ticking in the boot, Boss,' wailed Spider, his grin rapidly fading.

'In the boot!' whimpered Moss as he fumbled with the door latch.

The watch ticked on.

'You brainless, bungling . . .' Moss began.

And at that precise moment, the car blew up into a thousand pieces.

5
Flight!

Robin had just reached home and was about to tell his mother about the two sinister strangers when he was interrupted by the boom of the explosion. The whole house shook for a moment and further down the street several windows were broken. Mrs West thought that someone's boiler must have blown up, though Robin feared something worse, and they both ran into the street where already a big crowd had gathered.

Everything was in chaos. In the distance, the wail of police cars and the jangling of fire engines could be heard. At the top of Windsor Gardens, a great cloud of smoke was billowing around, only adding to the confusion. People were running up and down shouting. Several old age pensioners, thinking they were back in the war again, were looking for the nearest air-raid shelter. A stray dog was howling. And a traffic warden, who had had all her clothes torn off by the force of the explosion, was wandering about in a daze, trying to stick tickets on people.

Gradually news filtered back. The police arrived and discovered the wreck of the Mercedes. It seemed that a car had blown up, but by some miracle, nobody had been killed – though the two occupants had been rushed to hospital. The road was in a terrible mess, with glass and broken metal everywhere. Apparently a lamp-post had been blown out of the pavement like a rocket and had landed upside-down right through the roof of Mr Sylvester's grocery shop.

Somehow, amongst the smoke and the crowds and the police and the ambulance men, Robin managed to find his sister. Although she hadn't been hurt by the bomb, her face was blackened with soot and her dress had been torn. As soon as she saw Robin, she burst into tears.

'I'm a murderess,' she cried. 'I killed those two men.'

Robin held her close and told her that nobody had been killed. Then he managed to get the whole story out of her. It was obvious that the false uncles had indeed intended to kill him – but he was more puzzled than frightened. Who on earth would want to hurt him? It was true that he did have a few enemies. Mr Sylvester was one. And he had given the school bully a bleeding nose last term. Then there was his neighbour, and the unfortunate incident of the garden hut that had caught fire. But none of them would have gone to such extremes to get even with him . . .

'We can't tell anyone,' Mary said. 'They'd lock me up if they found out.'

'Don't be silly,' Robin said. 'It wasn't your fault. After all, you didn't make the bomb. You just delivered it. And if you hadn't been so sensible, it would have blown up the whole lot of us.'

Even so, they decided not to mention their own involvement in the explosion for the time being. You may think this a bit strange. But first of all, they didn't want to frighten their mother. And in spite of the certainty that it wasn't their fault, you must admit that it would be rather unusual for a twelve-year-old to

44

wander into a police station and say, 'Excuse me. I've just blown two people up and wrecked the High Street.'

No. They decided they would wait a little and see what developed. Perhaps the disaster of this second murder attempt would be the end of the matter. Besides, as Robin said, it wouldn't be long before the police realized that the poisoning one week and the explosion the next had to be connected.

Nonetheless, when the police finally did get to 64 Windsor Gardens again, it wasn't in the way that Robin and Mary had expected.

Frederick was having breakfast the next day when he heard the news on the radio of an explosion in Pinner. To the astonishment of his cook, who was just serving him a fifteenth rasher of bacon from a silver dish, he leapt out of his chair, grabbed Gervaise, and began to waltz around the room yelling 'They've done it!' at the top of his voice. Naturally, Frederick believed that Spider and Moss had carried out his orders successfully.

However, five minutes later the telephone rang and he heard about the unfortunate mistake. It was the head of Murder for Money & Company on the line, a woman by the name of Miss Crippen. She explained that somehow – she didn't know how exactly – her two top murderers had managed to blow themselves up and that the 'client' (meaning Robin) had escaped unhurt. However, she assured Frederick, as soon as Moss and Spider were out of hospital, they would try again at no extra charge.

'I promise you, we won't rest until we've given complete satisfaction,' the voice at the other end of the line trilled. Just remember our slogan.'

45

'And what's that?' Frederick demanded.

'We'll be the death of you.'

'Well you'd better get a move on,' Frederick snarled.

There was a click and the phone – at least – went dead.

For the rest of the morning, Frederick was in a frightful mood. He threw all the breakfast plates out of the window, stuck his tongue out at the cook, and sulked. He sulked for an hour, but even during that time his mind started ticking over various possibilities. It must be said that although Frederick was rotten at reading and writing, mouldy at maths, hopeless at history, feeble at French and useless at all the other subjects you learn at school, when it came to sheer nastiness, he was something of a genius. And now he had an idea.

He went back into the secret room and opened the filing cabinet marked 'Blackmail Victims', taking out the file on Chief Inspectors. This he read from cover to cover, smiling unpleasantly to himself. Then he picked up the telephone and dialled a number.

'Hello? Scotland Yard!' said a voice.

'I want to speak to Chief Inspector Hercule Crumb, the Head of Scotland Yard,' Frederick demanded.

'This is Hercule Crumb speaking,' said the voice. 'And from the sound of you, I would deduce that you are a twenty-seven-year-old woman with a slight limp who is missing some diamonds and that you want me to help you.'

'Wrong!' said Frederick. 'This is Frederick K. Bower.'

'Oh no!' the voice groaned.

'I want to see you, Crumb. Be here in ten minutes.'

'I'm busy,' Crumb said.

'I've found your file,' Frederick replied, slamming the phone down so hard that he broke it in half.

The story that Frederick had found in Crumb's file, and which enabled him to order the Chief of Scotland Yard around in this manner, was a rather sordid one. For twenty years, Hercule Crumb had lived with a guilty secret. When he was young and still a very junior policeman with a beat in Soho, he had started going to one of those seedy clubs that can be found in the area. The club was called 'The Sweaty Jumper', and Crumb had passed many a happy hour sitting there, drinking lemonade and watching ladies dancing without many clothes on.

Hercule Crumb had fallen in love with one of these ladies – a dancer by the name of Lola. As well as dancing, she sang rude songs and did unusual things with a pair of Wellington boots. Eventually Crumb had married her. She had given up her job and if anybody ever asked her what she had done before they met, she would answer that she had worked as a nurse. If it was discovered that a policeman, senior or junior, had gone to such disgraceful clubs and had actually married one of the performers, it would, of course, have been the end of his career.

This was Hercule Crumb's guilty secret, known only to himself and to Lola Crumb. Until Sir Montague had found out about it. Since then, Sir Montague had been blackmailing Crumb, making him turn a blind eye to some of the more illegal dealings of Bower Constructors, and generally upsetting the Chief of Police.

For otherwise, Crumb was a perfectly honest, hard-working policeman, even though in his whole life he

47

had never actually caught a single criminal. Although he did try very hard, the fact of the matter is that he was absolutely useless. He would look around for clues, ask questions, have a little drink, and then come to a deduction which was always, without fail, entirely wrong.

When Crumb arrived at Frederick's house, he was ushered into the study by Gervaise. Frederick was sitting behind the desk waiting for him, sucking a lollipop.

'I would deduce,' Crumb said, 'that you have asked me here on account of a recent visit made to you by a one-eyed dwarf from Bolivia who wishes to marry your aunt.'

'Incredible!' Frederick exclaimed. 'I don't know how you do it, Crumb. You're wrong again!'

'Then what do you want me for?' Crumb demanded. 'I thought I'd heard the last of the Bower family.'

'Temper, temper, Crumb,' Frederick muttered. 'And on the subject of families, how's Lola?'

'You leave my wife out of this, you wretch,' Crumb cried.

'If you call me names, I might just ring the Sunday newspapers about her,' Frederick said.

'Wait a minute . . .' Crumb began, going pale.

'Don't worry, Crumb,' Frederick interrupted. 'It's all right. As a matter of fact, the only reason I called you here is because I want to help you.'

'Help *me*?' Crumb said.

'Yes. I heard on the radio about the explosion in Pinner.'

'My men are investigating it now,' Crumb said. 'From what I've heard, I suspect the involvement of a group of Serbo-Croats, dedicated to the destruction of the world.'

'Wrong again!' Frederick said. 'But I can help you. I have inside information, you see.'

'Go on,' Crumb said.

'There is a boy living in Pinner. He's called Robin West . . .'

'He was involved in a recent poisoning,' Crumb recalled.

'He poisoned the burglar. And now he's blowing people up.'

'But he's only twelve!' Crumb exclaimed.

'He's started young,' Frederick said. 'And who knows where he'll stop?'

'My God!' Crumb whispered. 'Are you sure?'

'Certain,' Frederick replied. 'And if you don't hurry, he'll escape. You've go to lock him up in prison for ever and ever. You'd better leave straight away.'

Crumb stood up, knocking over his chair in his excitement. 'Thank you, Frederick,' he said. 'It's very decent of you to tell me this.'

'I'm just doing my duty, Crumb,' Frederick replied. 'Now, off you go.'

Crumb raced to the door. As he opened it, Frederick stopped him.

'Oh, if I were you,' he added, 'I'd make sure that all your police officers are equipped with guns. Shoot on sight if you have to. This boy is dangerous.'

'So it's agreed then. We'll go straight to the police station after tea, and tell them exactly what happened.'

Mary nodded. She and Robin were sitting in their bedroom, unknown to their mother who thought they were at the local cinema. But although they hadn't told her, neither of them had felt like seeing a film. They were far too worried, and had spent the whole day talking about their predicament.

But now that they'd come to a sensible decision, they both felt a lot more relieved.

'It's an end to our problems,' Robins said.

He was wrong. Their problems were only just beginning, for at that very same moment the police arrived.

One moment the street was deserted. Then, suddenly, with a screech of tyres and a wailing of sirens, the house was surrounded. No less than ten police cars screamed to a halt in front of 64 Windsor Gardens. Police vans threw open their doors and men wearing bullet-proof clothing and carrying rifles leapt into the road and ran for cover. Marksmen climbed on to the roofs of local houses. Police dogs howled, straining at the leash, hoping to get their teeth into some unfortunate criminal.

In less than a minute, the whole street had been roped off. Everything was quiet but for the snarling of the dogs. Then Chief Inspector Hercule Crumb stepped forward. Twenty rifles were cocked to cover him. Slowly, he lifted a loud-speaker.

'Robin West!' he shouted. 'This is the police. We know you're in there. Your house is surrounded. You haven't got a chance. Come out with your hands above your head, very slowly. You have exactly one minute or we'll be forced to open fire.'

Inside the house, Robin and Mary, who had seen the police arrive from an upstairs window, went as white as chalk. Robin was speechless. He couldn't move, he was so frightened. Every muscle in his body had turned to jelly. Thirty seconds – it seemed like an hour – passed. Then the front door opened and Mrs West, who had been in the kitchen, stepped out on to the pavement.

'Hello?' she said, not quite believing her eyes and quite certain that she was dreaming.

'I deduce,' shouted Crumb as he dived for cover behind a car, 'I deduce that you are the leader of the gang and a dangerous criminal.'

'How dare you!' Mrs West retorted. 'I am Robin's mother, Mrs West. Do you want to see him?'

'Is he inside?' Crumb asked.

'No. He's gone to the cinema,' Mrs West replied. This is what Robin had told her.

'The cinema!' Crumb cried. 'Come on, men! We'll go and surround the cinema. With a bit of luck we'll even get to see some of the cartoon.'

And with a renewed screech of tyres, a baying of hounds, a shouting of orders, a shrieking of whistles and a roar of engines, the policemen all rushed off to surround the local cinema. Mrs West, still quite sure that she was asleep and having a dream, went back into the kitchen to continue making her chocolate stew and steak and kidney mousse.

Upstairs, Robin and Mary stared at each other in horror. What would you do if there had been two attempts on your life by a mysterious enemy and you were suddenly wanted by the police for a crime you hadn't committed? There wasn't even that much time to think about it, for as soon as the police discovered that their suspect wasn't in the cinema, they would be back in a flash for sure.

'We've got to get out of here,' Robin said.

51

'Run away?' Mary asked.

'What else can we do?'

The truth is, they were so shocked by the events of the past week that they were completely unable to reason the whole thing out. For Robin, the thought of being arrested, handcuffed and locked in a van, with all the neighbours watching and probably laughing at his expense, was too awful to think about. As for Mary, she wouldn't have dreamt of leaving her brother to run away by himself. So without any more ado, the two crept down the stairs and tip-toed past the kitchen, where Mrs West was singing merrily, having already forgotten about the police. Seeing her handbag in the hall, Robin did something which he had never done before. He took five pounds out without asking her.

However, before he left, he did write a hurried note. This is what the note said.

Dearest Mother,

Mary and I are honestly innocent, but I can't bear the thought of being arrested for something I didn't do. So we've run away and we're not coming back until we find out what's going on.

Love,

Robin.

PS I have borrowed five pounds from your handbag.

PPS Don't worry!

He put the note on the table where their mother would be sure to find it. Then he and Mary slipped out into the street. Fortunately, there was nobody about.

But he had hardly taken two steps before the noise of approaching sirens warned him that the police were already on their way back. Hand in hand, Robin and

Mary turned down the nearest alleyway and then ran as fast as their feet could carry them.

Where were they going? Just then, neither of them knew. All they wanted to do was to get as far away from 64 Windsor Gardens as they possible could.

6
Wanted!

Two hours after Robin and Mary had fled, Mrs West's house was being turned upside-down. There were policemen in every room, opening cupboards and drawers, tearing pillow cases into shreds, sniffing the sugar and uprooting the plants in their search for clues. Amid great clouds of powder, finger-print men examined every inch of the furniture for finger-prints. There were journalists and newspaper photographers everywhere, shouting questions and flashing camera bulbs. Some of the neighbours, including Mr Sylvester, had dropped in to see what was going on and were tramping all over the clean carpets with their dirty feet.

And, in the middle of it all, sat Mrs West. She was utterly confused by the events as nobody had had the time to explain everything to her. She was sitting in an armchair with a hot cup of tea. She clutched a damp slice of bread, which she had mistaken for a handkerchief, in one hand.

'Tell us about your son,' cried the journalists.

But Mrs West just burst into tears.

'*The mother who weeps for her boy . . .*' wrote the journalists.

'The little rascal tried to lock me in the deep freeze,' shouted Mr Sylvester, who wanted to get his name in the papers.

'*Attempted to kill the local grocer,*' wrote the journalists.

'And he sent the vicar the News of the World instead of the Church Gazette,' Mr Sylvester added.

'*Vicar in shock horror nude photograph scandal,*' wrote the journalists.

'He isn't any naughtier than any other boy of his age,' Mrs West muttered.

'*Naughtier than any other boy of his age,*' the journalists quoted.

'Boys like West deserve a good caning,' Mr Sylvester snarled. 'In fact, I'd cane him myself given half a chance. Caning is good for you. Would anyone like to see my collection of canes?'

Only one week before, Robin West had been an ordinary, cheerful, twelve-year-old boy. But, by the time the journalists had asked all their questions (and drunk all the whisky in the house) and by the time the first editions of the evening papers were rolling out of the press, he was the most wanted and the most dangerous person in the whole country.

Following their narrow escape from the police in Pinner, Robin and Mary had run all the way to the nearest Underground Station and had bought two single tickets to Piccadilly Circus. Piccadilly Circus is slap bang in the middle of the great city of London, and in their intial panic, they had decided that they would have the least chance of being spotted if they lost themselves amongst the thousands of people that they would find there.

It was only when they emerged into the middle of Piccadilly that such problems as where they would

55

spend the night – with only a little over four pounds between them – and how they would find their way around such a huge place occurred to them.

After the peace and quiet of the suburbs, London was a nightmare. Cars seemed to pile up on them from all sides. Hundreds and hundreds of people bustled along the dirty pavements, an endless flood that seemed to be flowing in every direction but going nowhere. It was already growing dark and vast neon lights had sprung into life, advertising drinks and cigarettes with flickering patterns. Shifty characters had set up little stalls in the street, selling cheap trinkets and souvenirs. Leather-jacketed punks shuffled past, blank-eyed and vaguely menacing behind their garish hair colours and make-up. Long-haired tramps and hippies sat amid piles of litter, smoking and drinking from concealed bottles in creased paper bags.

Obviously the first thing they had to do was to find a hotel for the night. But Robin and Mary were sadly ignorant of London hotels. They tramped around Piccadilly for hours, but without any luck. If they were able to get past the hostile doormen and suspicious receptionists, they found that a room would cost them sixty, seventy, even a hundred pounds for the night. Their four single pound notes, which had seemed like a lot of money, proved to be worth nothing at all.

By a quarter to ten, they were exhausted and ravenously hungry. They now found themselves in Leicester Square, a few minutes from Piccadilly Circus, but equally unpleasant. Above their heads, thousands of pigeons were settling down for the night, whistling and whooping in a ghostly way.

'Let's get something to eat,' Robin said.

'Where?' Mary was close to tears.

'We can get a hamburger. We've got to have enough money for that.'

There was a fast-food restaurant nearby and soon they were being served luke-warm hamburgers, boxes of greasy chips and sluggish milk-shakes.

'Have a nice day,' the counter girl said.

'Terrific,' Robin muttered.

He counted his change. They had just seventeen pence left.

They ate slowly, too tired to notice the food, which tasted about as good as the containers it was served in. Neither of them dared ask what they were going to do next. The whole adventure had gone terribly wrong. It seemed that the only answer was to go back to Pinner and give themselves up.

Sitting at the table next to them, a rather ugly woman in a tight dress and with too much lip-stick was idly reading the Evening Standard. From the way that she glanced at everyone who came into the restaurant, it looked as if she was waiting for someone. But Robin noticed that as he sat down near her, she had suddenly frowned and turned back to the front page of the paper.

Out of the corner of his eye, Robin glanced at the newspaper, wondering what should have upset the woman. And this is what he saw:

WANTED

Police today began a massive man-hunt for 12-year-old Robin West who, it is claimed, is the most dangerous person in England. Chief Inspector Crumb, who is in charge of the case, described the boy as a 'maniac'. Asked if the West boy was violent, he added, 'He makes the Kray Brothers look about as deadly as Sooty & Sweep'.

In an astonishing police-raid on 64 Windsor Gardens, Pinner, this afternoon, Robin West, wanted for poisoning a burglar, blowing up a Mercedes with the occupants inside, attempting to murder a local shop-keeper, vandalism, shop-lifting, arson and for sending rude photographs to the vicar, just managed to escape. He has taken his 11-year-old sister, Mary, with him as a hostage, and is believed to have headed for London.

REWARD
Speaking from his headquarters at Bower Constructors House, Frederick Kenneth Bower has offered a £10,000 reward and a life-supply of lollipops to the person caturing Robin West.

Mr Bower told reporters: 'I have a duty to protect London people from this nasty little crook. People like Robin West ought to be sent to prison for ever and ever.' Mr Bower is twelve and a half.

'Mary?' Robin whispered.
    'What is it?' Mary sighed, yawning.
    'Look at the newspaper!'
    Mary followed his eye and gasped in spite of herself. The first thing she saw was Robin's photograph and the word 'Wanted'. Then, before she could read anything more, the woman had whisked the paper away, and was standing up, clearly alarmed.
    'I think we'd better get out of here,' Robin whispered.
    But even as he moved, the woman, who must have thought that Robin was going to attack her, suddenly started screaming.

58

'Police! Police! For Gawd's sake 'elp me!' she screeched.

And to make matters worse, two police constables who had been sipping coffee at the counter, immediately started walking towards her to see what all the fuss was about.

Robin and Mary dashed out into the street and would have got clean away had not a spirited Londoner grabbed them from behind, believing that they were trying to get out of the restaurant without paying.

'What do you think you're up to . . .' he began. Then he saw Robin's face and let go of him as if he had been made of red-hot steel. 'Blimey!' he shouted. 'It's Robin West!' and immediately fainted.

Before the two policemen could reach them, a small crowd had completely surrounded the children.

'Mon dieu! Sacre bleu!' a Frenchman was crying excitedly.

'Donner und Blitzen!' shouted a German tourist as he tried to take a photograph of the scene.

'Hey! Wait until I tell the kids about this!' exclaimed an American lady as she was trampled underfoot by the excited crowd.

'Keep away!' shouted the police, who had found out what was happening. 'It's the loony from Pinner. He's dangerous!'

At the word 'dangerous', the crowd started shrieking with fear, which only made matters worse as the noise quickly attracted more people to the scene. Soon the whole corner of Leicester Square was packed with people who, having fought their way to the centre of attraction, were now trying to fight their way out of it again. Clothes were ripped in the general panic. A wig

59

went flying through the air, followed, a moment later, by its owner. Several more people fainted. The two policemen had started blowing their whistles, and soon a whole lot more policemen had joined in the fray.

Then suddenly, a woman called out, 'There they go!' Everyone stopped fighting for a moment and turned to gaze at a street running off the square. And there indeed were Robin and Mary who had escaped in all the confusion and were in full flight.

The chase was on! No fewer than sixteen policemen started off in pursuit, followed by an immense crowd, all of whom were hoping to win the £10,000 promised by Frederick. An entire coachload of Japanese tourists, seeing the blue police uniforms flash past them, joined in the chase, although they didn't know what was going on, and even a one-man-band, who had been playing to a cinema audience, ran behind everyone else, jingling, crashing and tooting as he went.

Robin and Mary were so frightened that they ran faster than they would ever have believed possible. They came to a main road and without looking left or right dashed straight across. A taxi skidded to avoid them and with a great 'Zing' of broken glass drove straight into a shop window.

A minute later, the sixteen policemen, the crowd, the Japanese tourists and the one-man-band were streaking over the main road, leaping over the bits of broken glass. A Rolls Royce, whose licence plate was FKB 5 was forced to swerve, mounted the pavement and disappeared down the steps of an Underground Station with a dreadful rattling and grinding of metal. There were angry cries and even a small fight in one part of the road. But still Mary and Robin ran on.

Now they followed twisting side-streets, turning left at one and right at the next in an attempt to lose their pursuers. Yet even as they ran, the police were calling for assistance over their portable radios, and more policemen were rushing to the scene. Roads all round the area were being blocked off, quickly and efficiently. Believe it or not, five hundred policemen and three crack regiments from the SAS were called into the heart of London that night to try to trap Robin and Mary.

It was eleven o'clock now and, as it happened, the evening's opera at Covent Garden had just ended. A crowd of very elegant people, the men dressed in dinner jackets and the women loaded down by heavy pieces of jewellery, were just coming out of the theatre, chatting excitedly and whistling the tunes, when Robin and Mary appeared and began to push their way through.

'Steady on!' someone said.

'How fraffly rude!' said someone else.

But for the opera-goers, the interruption was only just beginning. No sooner had Robin and Mary disappeared down another side-street than someone cried, 'I say, there are sixteen policemen rushing towards us.'

'I say,' said another person.

'Aaargh!' cried an elderly lady as the leading policeman accidentally knocked her over.

'Sorry mum!' the policeman said.

'I'm not your mum!' the lady replied. 'I'm the Duchess of Devonshire, and I'd be jolly grateful if you'd take your foot out of my ear.'

But by now the police were charging through the crowd, barging into people and generally causing a dreadful disturbance. Diamonds and rubies flew in all directions, to the delight of the one-man-band who was making enough noise to awaken the dead in his hurry to pick them up. In all the confusion, a telephone box was upturned, a street cleaner was swept away and two policemen managed to arrest each other.

But the opera-goers had held up their pursuers long enough for Robin and Mary to get away. When they stopped for breath, the road behind them was empty and they could hear the shouts of the crowd going off in the wrong direction. They had run nearly a mile by now and they were close to exhaustion.

'Which way?' Mary panted.

'Over the bridge,' Robin wheezed. 'We may be safer on the other side of the river.'

The bridge they had come to was called Waterloo Bridge. Although it is true that it led out of the centre of London across the River Thames, it was not at all a good idea to try to cross it. For a start, it was very wide and modern, and there was no way they could avoid being seen on it. And secondly, although they didn't know it, the SAS had set up a block on the far side. There were three jeeps, side by side, fifteen soldiers, all carrying automatic rifles, and even a tank, its cannon pointing towards the north bank.

It was only when Robin and Mary were half way across, suspended high above the cold waters of the River Thames, that they saw that their way was blocked.

'We're finished!' Mary cried.

'Let's turn back,' Robin said.

'We can't. Look!'

Robin turned round to face the way he had just

come, and saw the most extraordinary sight. Two men, one fat, the other thin, and both completely wrapped up in bandages like Egyptian mummies, were slowly driving towards them in electric wheel-chairs. The fat one was clutching a sub-machine gun. The thin one carried a handful of grenades.

These two men, as you may well have guessed, were none other than Spider and Moss Kito, who had been bandaged up to recover from the explosion of their Mercedes. Although they had been confined to neighbouring beds in a hospital near Covent Garden, they had heard on the news that the two children had been sighted in the area. They had immediately heaved themselves out of bed and, as they were still unable to walk, had stolen two electric wheel-chairs from an astonished nurse, and had motored out on to the streets of London. They had been fortunate enough to spot Robin almost immediately as he escaped through the opera crowd, and it was they who had misled the pursuing policemen. They were determined to finish off the job which they had started.

So it was that Robin and Mary found themselves trapped in the middle of Waterloo Bridge. On one side were the crack regiments of the SAS who couldn't wait to get cracking and demolish them. On the other side, the world's two most deadly assassins were slowly wheeling towards them, weapons poised.

'We're done for,' Robin cried.

'It was nice knowing you,' Mary said.

'I'm sorry this had to happen,' Robin muttered.

And they both closed their eyes and waited for their terrible end.

It was then that it happened.

A loud hooting from the far side of the bridge made the SAS men swing round and then leap aside to avoid being run over. Suddenly a motor-bike, with a side-car attached, had burst on to the bridge, crashing through the barrier. It was driven by a figure dressed entirely in black leather from tip to toe. The leather suit had silver studs on the back and chains hanging from the front. The figure wore a black helmet with a black glass visor, so it would impossible for anyone to describe whoever it was driving the bike.

The motor-bike zoomed pass the flabbergasted SAS men and before anyone could do anything it had pulled up beside Robin and Mary.

'Get in – quick!' a voice commanded.

Not knowing what he was letting himself in for, Robin (who had opened his eyes), pulled Mary into the side-car and got in himself. Immediately, the strange figure accelerated and the three of them shot away from the SAS blockade and towards Spider and Moss, who were still approaching in their wheel-chairs.

'Get out of the way!' Spider shouted.

'Look out, you nincompoop,' hissed Moss, as their wheel-chairs collided, sparks flying from the engines.

And then the motor-bike burst right through the middle of them and before Spider or Moss could control them, their motorized wheel-chairs began madly spinning round and round before sailing off the side of the bridge with the two invalids still inside them. For a moment, the wheel-chairs hung in mid-air, still turning round, and then with one last cry, Spider and Moss plunged into the freezing, dirty waters of the River Thames, disappearing in a whirlpool of bubbles.

But before they had even hit the water, the motorbike had roared away into the distance. Robin and Mary gripped on to the sides, afraid for their very lives. Sixty, seventy, eighty miles an hour, the motorbike sped on. The mysterious driver ignored red traffic lights, pedestrians and other cars. They went across roundabouts instead of round them, flew under bridges and round corners and even raced along the pavement at times, often balancing on one wheel. Robin and Mary were so scared that they quite forgot that they had just been saved from both the SAS and the assassins.

After twenty minutes, the bike suddenly stopped and with a quick bound the driver got off. Trembling all over, Robin and Mary got out and breathed a sigh of relief to find themselves standing safely on the firm ground.

'Thank you . . .' Robin began, but then stopped dead in absolute amazement as the driver removed the black helmet.

Their rescuer was a woman. And one of the oldest women Robin had ever seen.

7

Unfair Exchange

Have you ever woken up in a strange bed, in a strange house, and wondered where you are and how you even got there? That's what happened to Mary the next morning when she opened her eyes. She was lying tucked up in a somewhat small but very comfortable bunk, about six feet off the floor, and from his snoring, she could tell that Robin was in the bunk beneath her.

The first thing she saw was a small porthole right next to her head, with two lace-curtains half-drawn across it. Opening her eyes a little wider, she found herself in an extremely unusual room. It had curving walls, and was shaped more like a circle than the square you would expect a bedroom to be. Furthermore, there was only a narrow passage between the bunk and the table against the opposite wall, and there was scarcely enough space for the two chairs on which their clothes were hanging.

It was a boat. She was sure that the strange old lady had stopped her motorbike beside a boat. But as far as she could remember, they were nowhere near the River Thames and they couldn't have driven as far as the coast. She felt for any rocking movement, but there was none. Beneath her, Robin gave a loud sniff and woke up.

'Mary?' he asked after a minute.

'Yes?'

'Where are you?'

'I'm above you,' Mary said, hanging upside-down over the side of her bunk so that she could see her brother.

'Are we on a boat?' Robin asked.

'I think so,' Mary said. 'But the boat doesn't seem to be on any water.'

'I love boats. But I hate water.'

The voice came from the open door of the bedroom, and there stood the old lady who had rescued them the night before. 'Welcome to my boat, *Dunsailin*,' she trilled. 'All my life I wanted to have my own little boat. I love boats. Always have. But I hate water. Nasty wet stuff.'

'Are we in a field then?' Mary asked as she tried to look out of the window.

'Good heavens, no!' the old lady replied. 'There aren't many fields left in London now – thanks to Bower Constructors and the like. No. We're near Paddington Station.'

'Do you mean this boat is parked in a road?' Robin asked as politely as he could.

'So many questions before breakfast!' the old lady cried. 'Come on now. It's well past nine-thirty and it's unhealthy to stay in bed too long. I've cleaned and dried your clothes, so hurry up and get dressed and come into the galley for breakfast.'

And with that, she vanished again in the direction from which she had come. A moment later, a delicious smell of eggs and bacon began to fill the air, and Robin and Mary got dressed as quickly as possible.

Outside their bedroom, they came across a flight of stairs going upwards and, following the smell, they climbed them and found themselves in a beautiful living room. The walls were curved, like the bedroom, but this room was much bigger. There was a lovely old rocking chair next to a fireplace in which a fire had already been lit, though it wasn't very cold. All the windows had hand-made lace curtains and there were flower pots everywhere. The armchairs were those big old-fashioned sort with floral patterns and fat cushions that it's a delight to sink into. Everything was neat and tidy. But for the shape of the walls, you would never guess that you were on a boat.

Next to the living room was a small dining-room with three chairs around a wooden table, which was already laden with everything you could possibly want for breakfast. There were four different types of cereal and a big jug of milk, hot rolls, hot toast, freshly squeezed orange juice and every variety of jam including Dandelion and Thistle. Also, which was rather peculiar, there were little bottles of pills and medicines all over the place. They all had labels reading 'Vitamin A', 'B', or 'C', 'Syrup for Colds', 'Embrocation for Rheumatism' and so on. With this curious mixture, the room looked like a cross between a food-shop and a chemist.

Attached to the dining-room was the kitchen, or 'galley' as the lady had called it. Their hostess was standing in this room, bending over a vast old-fashioned stove, shuffling an enormous copper frying-pan around. Inside the pan, Robin and Mary could see eggs, bacon, mushrooms, kidneys, sausages and fried bread.

For the first time, they could examine their rescuer more closely. She really was very old – at least ninety, though her face was full of colour and her eyes twinkled mischievously. She had silver hair, wrapped in tight curls, and she wore a pair of pince-nez, which are spectacles that hang on your nose without the bits that go behind your ears. She was wearing a tartan frock which was either too long for her or too short, but certainly not quite right, and a baggy jumper which hung on her like an over-emotional sheep.

'There you are!' the old lady said when she saw Robin and Mary. 'Sit down and have a dose of Syrup of Figs before breakfast! Or perhaps you would prefer orange juice? Full of Vitamin C!'

Robin and Mary quickly poured themselves some orange juice.

'It was very kind of you to rescue us . . .' Robin began, wondering what he should call the woman.

'Call me Meg! Everyone does, even though it isn't my name at all!' the woman said. 'And I shall call you Robin and Mary. You *are* Robin and Mary West, I presume?'

'Yes,' Mary assured her.

'How awful it would be if I had rescued the wrong people. Oh dear me yes!' and she burst into a fit of laughter. 'Oh dear!' she said, pulling a lace handkerchief from her sleeve and dabbing at her eyes. 'I really shouldn't laugh so much. I'm sure it isn't good for me.'

Naturally, Robin wanted to ask Meg all sorts of questions. Who was she? Why had she rescued them? Did she know anything about the chocolates? But she refused to have any such discussion over the table.

'Breakfast first. Business later,' she said, as she served up huge portions from the copper pan.

At last, when Robin and Mary were absolutely full

and had assured her that they couldn't manage even a sip more tea, she cleared the table and led her guests into the living-room.

The fire was blazing merrily as she installed herself in the rocking chair and motioned Robin and Mary to sit down. Robin was about to plop himself down on a furry cushion, when a sudden squeak warned him that it wasn't a cushion but a cat. The old lady roared with laughter.

'People are always sitting on Sophocles,' she cried. 'Come here, Sophocles!'

And the cat, which seemed to be as old as Meg, and which squeaked like a mouse instead of purring like a cat, waddled over and clambered into her lap where it promptly fell asleep.

Then she made Robin and Mary tell her their story right from the beginning, stopping them whenever they missed out even the slightest detail. She asked what was the maker's name on the chocolates and frowned when Mary mentioned the name of Bower. She seemed puzzled about the involvement of the police and the SAS and the story in the newspaper, and she was so excited by the account of the chase through London that she nearly fell out of the rocking-chair.

Finally, when she had heard everything that they could tell her, she got up and poked the fire and fed Sophocles a small piece of cheese, and then sat in silence for a full minute.

'Now I shall tell you my story,' she said suddenly. 'The shadows of the past have caught up with us at last. I warn you, though, there are a number of shocks in store for you. And particularly you!' She pointed at Robin.

'Why me?' Robin asked.

'Tell me,' Meg replied, 'do you know . . . do you know who your real parents are?'

'Well,' Robin said, 'I know I was adopted, if that's what you mean. But I never knew my real parents.'

'That makes things easier,' Meg muttered. 'Now listen carefully.'

And this is what she told them.

'Many years ago, before Mary was even born, there was a very, very rich and very unpleasant man called Sir Montague Bower. He made his fortune by starting a company called Bower Constructors, which builds things and owns shops and restaurants.'

'Bowers Chocolates!' Robin exclaimed.

'Exactly. Sir Montague was married to a vain and foolish woman called Lady Penelope who gave birth to a child, a boy. Now, in the ward next to Lady Penelope, another woman gave birth to another boy. She was called Ruby Sponge and the boy was christened Robin.'

'I'm confused,' Mary said.

'It gets worse.' Meg smiled. 'All right – there were two babies: Frederick Bower and Robin Sponge. Frederick was born into a world of great wealth and comfort. His parents had millions. But for Robin it was an altogether different matter.

'His mother, Ruby, was a poor, sickly creature. She lived in a horrible flat with no corners because it had – by coincidence – been built by Bower Constructors. The roof leaked and there were mushrooms growing on the carpets. But the worst thing about Ruby was her husband. She had married a brute, a real monster. He drove a taxi cab when he wasn't drunk, but as he

71

was drunk nearly all the time, he never made much money.'

'How do you know all this?' Robin asked.

Meg sighed. 'Because I was Ruby's great aunt. I warned her against the marriage, but the truth is, nobody ever listened to me. They all thought I was mad. And perhaps, in a way, they were right . . .

'You see, I was working as a nurse in the hospital, and one of the doctors told me about Frederick K. Bower. And then a thought came into my mind. It was a wicked thought, a mad thought. But I was young at the time . . . in my early seventies . . . and I didn't know better. I thought to myself, why should my great great-nephew, Robin, grow up poor and miserable when this other boy, this Frederick, has all the money in the world? And then I thought that it was all luck anyway and that but for a blink in God's eye, Robin could just as well have ended up in Frederick's cot and Frederick in Robin's. And then I thought a bit more, and then . . .'

'You swapped the babies!' Mary gasped.

'Yes, Mary. It was a dreadful thing to do, but I waited until nobody was looking and I swapped them. And as one baby looks very much like another, nobody noticed.

'It took me about forty-eight hours to come to my senses and at once I wrote to Sir Montague. I didn't tell him who I was, but I told him what I'd done. He didn't reply. So I wrote again, this time enclosing my great, great-nephew's birth certificate. The baby Robin had been born with a birth-mark on one shoulder, a birth-mark that his Frederick now carried. Still he refused to reply.

'In the end I managed to get him on the telephone. And then he told me the terrible truth. He didn't want his baby back.'

'Why not?' Mary asked.

'Because he was happy with the baby he'd got and didn't particularly care whose it was. At least, that's what he said. But I think there was something else. He was afraid . . . afraid of being made a fool of. If the story had come out, it would have been in all the newspapers . . .'

'Couldn't you have swapped the two babies back again without anyone noticing?' Robin asked.

Meg shook her head. 'No. You see, in the meantime, something else had happened. Ruby Sponge had decided to leave her husband and emigrate to Australia. And she had left her baby behind at the hospital who had immediately arranged for it to be adopted. There was no way I could get anywhere near it.'

'And who adopted the baby?' Robin asked, but already he knew the answer.

'You were that baby, Robin.' Meg explained. 'You were the original Frederick K. Bower. And it was your mother, Mrs West, who adopted you.'

'What!' Mary exclaimed.

'Then I . . .' Robin began.

'Yes,' Meg exclaimed. 'You are the real heir to the millions which Sir Montague left when he accidentally got crushed last year. Don't you see? Somehow the second Frederick has found out about the baby-swap, and that's why he's so anxious to be rid of you, in case you find out about it too!'

'But how could he have found out?' Robin said.

'Perhaps he found the original letters and the birth

certificate,' Meg said. 'Or he could have found the letter which I wrote later on . . .'

'What letter was that?' Mary asked.

Meg sighed again. 'Ever since I did that stupid thing, I've tried to make up for it,' she said. 'I went to work for Sir Montague and became one of the nannies who looked after his new baby. I was known as Nanny Sniff and I was supposed to be in charge of his health. It was the only way I could be near my great, great-nephew and perhaps make sure he was brought up properly. But, of course, I failed. He grew up to be a little monster.

'And at the same time, I wrote again to Sir Montague. I often used to pass through Pinner, just to catch sight of you, and I knew how difficult things were for you. So I asked Sir Montague to send you some money, to buy you some of the things you needed. I mean, it was after all rightfully yours. I even sent him a photograph of you. I thought when he saw what a handsome child you had become, he would be moved to pity. But once again he ignored me.'

Mary and Robin were speechless. The whole story was so utterly incredible that at first they thought that Meg must be making it up. But it did make sense. The chocolates had come from Fortnum and Bower. It was Frederick Bower who had offered a reward for Robin's arrest in the Evening Standard. And what other reason could there be for the appearance of the two assassins?'

At last Mary turned to her brother. 'You're a millionaire!' she exclaimed. 'A multi-millionaire, and you never knew it until now. Golly, Robin . . . or I suppose I ought to call you Frederick . . .'

'Don't you dare!' Robin said. 'My name is Robin

74

West. I think Frederick Kenneth is a perfectly horrid name – even if that's what I was really christened.'

'What are you going to do with all the money?' Mary asked.

But the truth is, Robin hadn't even begun to think what it would mean. Obviously one or two small things flashed across his mind. The hall needed a new carpet. He and Mary could both buy new bicycles. They could get their mother a fantastic Christmas present. But when you're talking about millions and millions of pounds, these considerations are mere trifles. And there was still too much to be done before he could claim what was really his.

'Why didn't you tell me about this years ago?' he asked.

'I never meant to tell you about it at all,' Meg said. 'I never would have if Frederick hadn't forced my hand. Having lots and lots of money isn't very nice, you know.'

'I wouldn't mind,' Mary said.

'But what about all the taxes?' Meg continued. 'What about the accountants and the bankers always pestering you? And all the crooked, greedy people flattering you and trying to swindle you? Money has a funny way of changing people for the worse. I mean . . . look what it's done for Frederick.'

'I haven't even got the money yet,' Robin said, 'and already I feel a bit gloomy. What are we going to do?'

Meg stroked Sophocles who squeaked contentedly. 'We can't go to the police,' she said. 'They wouldn't believe us – and besides, you two are still wanted criminals. No. The first thing we've got to do is to find proof of what's been going on.'

'The birth certificate!' Mary exclaimed.

'Exactly,' Meg said. 'Frederick must have found it and I'll bet he's hidden it somewhere. Rich and important people seldom destroy papers. They like to keep them in secret places in case they ever have need of them.'

'But how can we find out where they are?'

Carrying Sophocles, Meg got out of her rocking chair and went over to the table. She picked up a copy of the Evening Standard, the same editon that had Robin's photograph on the front page, and thumbed through it until she arrived at the Jobs Section. She spread it out in front of them and there, circled in red, was an advertisement.

LIFT PERSON REQUIRED

Bower Constructors Limited, the well-known building company, is looking for a young person to replace their lift-boy who has been fired for trying to make the lift go sideways. This is a very good job with lots of opportunity to go up in the world (as well as down).

We will pay £25.00 a week, and other benefits include lots of lollipops and a free, framed photograph of our chairman, F. K. Bower Esq. Apply to Mr Toadwell at New Bower House, Bower Street, London W1.

'You've got to apply for the job,' Meg said to Robin when he had read the advertisement.

'But why?' Robin said. 'I don't want to work in New Bower House.'

'Don't you see?' Meg exclaimed. 'If you can get into the headquarters of the Bower Empire, you may be able to overhear things – slip into offices and discover things.'

'But won't they recognize him?' Mary asked.

'I'll see to that,' Meg replied. 'We'll colour his hair or get him a wig and he can wear false spectacles. And I'll paint a wart on his nose. If it's a big enough wart, nobody will look at anything else.'

'It sounds exciting,' Robin said.

'Exciting?' Meg turned away and a cloud must have passed in front of the sun for it was suddenly dark in the boat. 'You have to find that certificate, Robin,' she said. 'And you don't have much time. Frederick is looking for you. Even now he's looking for you.

'And once he finds you . . . you're dead.'

8

Murder for Money

Chief Inspector Hercule Crumb was perplexed.

He was sitting behind his untidy desk in his untidy office on the second floor of New Scotland Yard, furiously sucking chewing-gum. The walls of his office were cluttered up with photographs of all the most wanted criminals in Europe including Hans Upper, the German bank robber, Mark de Cards, the famous French cheat, Ali Bye, the Indian burglar and the Great Train Robbers (who had all been caught years ago, though somebody had forgotten to tell Crumb). And in the middle of them all, a photograph of Robin West, smiling innocently, had been pinned to the wall with a well-aimed dart.

'We've got to find him!' cried Crumb, pulling at his fingers until the bones clicked.

Opposite Crumb, and partially hidden by a cloud of grey smoke, sat his assistant whose name was Hackney. As policemen have a rather strange tendency to drop their aitches, he was known as Acne which is, by coincidence, a rather nasty disease from which he suffered. This may well have been caused by his smoking habits. Hackney smoked far too much. He smoked too much because he was worried. And he was worried because he smoked too much. Sometimes when he was particularly worried, he would light two cigarettes at a time. Not surprisingly, he was very short and coughed and wheezed quite appallingly.

'Find who?' Hackney asked in response to his boss's statement.

'Robin West, of course!' said Crumb, getting out of his chair and pacing over to a detailed map of London. The map was so full of red and green pins that it was impossible to see any of the streets.

'We know he's in London,' Crumb continued, going slightly red. 'But he's escaped from us twice. Twice, I tell you!' He went slightly more red. 'The whole of New Scotland Yard beaten twice by a twelve-year-old . . .'

Crumb was now writhing about and his face had gone bright crimson. At first Hackney assumed he was having a fit of rage, but in fact Crumb had swallowed his chewing-gum whole and was choking himself to death.

'Our men have searched the whole city,' Hackney said as the Chief of Police rolled about on the carpet, clutching at his throat. 'But he seems to have vanished without a trace. Are you all right, sir?'

Crumb sat up, and with a great 'Tcha-hoom!' managed to spit out the offending piece of gum. He then pulled the flowers out of a vase, drank all the water in one gulp, and threw himself back into his chair. Hackney, who was completely bewildered by this strange behaviour, lit another cigarette and coughed.

Finally Crumb spoke. 'Who was riding the motorbike which rescued the boy?' he asked.

'We don't know,' wheezed Hackney. 'It was a Japanese make, and it didn't have any number-plates.'

'I deduce, then,' Crumb said, 'that it was stolen by an extremely unpleasant Japanese airplane pilot or – to put it another way – a nasty nip in the air.'

79

'But most motor-bikes are made by the Japanese these days,' Hackney protested.

'Have you checked my theory, Acne?'

'No, sir,' Hackney sighed.

'Then do it!'

Hackney scribbled the order down on a note-pad and lit another cigarette without noticing the one already burning between his lips. The door opened and another, younger man walked in carrying a sheet of paper covered in typewriting.

'The latest report, sir,' he said, saluting, and left the two men together.

Crumb read the report, scowling. 'Dammit!' he said when he had finished. 'Look at this, Acne! This case becomes more and more complicated every minute. The two men who got blown up in the Mercedes in Pinner . . .'

'. . . and who later vanished from the hospital in two stolen wheel-chairs?' Hackney asked.

'The same two men,' Crumb snapped. 'Well, I've just received a report from our Records Office. Those two men were none other than Spider and Moss Kito, the two most dangerous assassins in the world!'

'Spider and Moss Kito!' Hackney whistled. 'I thought they had been eaten by cannibals on a mission in South Africa last year!'

'It seems that they survived,' Crumb deduced.

He began to pace around the office again, scratching his head and talking to himself.

'Let me think,' he said. 'Spider and Moss Kito, believed dead, are blown up in Pinner by Robin West who, it seems, had already poisoned Sam Fingers, a petty burglar. Now, why should this West child do that?'

'Perhaps he doesn't like criminals,' Hackney suggested.

'Don't we all, don't we all,' Crumb mused. 'But that doesn't mean we go around the place blowing them up, does it? And anyway, how would he know that Spider and Kito were criminals to begin with?'

'Search me,' Hackney said.

'Why? What have you hidden?' Crumb demanded.

'No, sir. I meant . . . I don't know.'

'Right. Now, when I last came across them, Spider and Moss were working for the deadly and top secret organization, Murder for Money & Company who, as you know, will kill anyone if the price is right.'

'Then surely,' Hackney coughed, 'Spider and Moss Kito were paid to kill Robin West rather than the other way round.'

'Are you suggesting that the bomb was intended for Robin West – but accidentally blew up the two assassins?' cried Crumb.

'Exactly!' Hackney replied, lighting yet another two cigarettes in the excitement of the moment.

'Brilliant!' Crumb exclaimed. 'How clever of me to think of it!'

'I thought of it!' Hackney complained.

'Are you arguing with a superior officer?' returned Crumb.

He sat down at the desk again and opened an already bulging file on Robin, adding the new report to the top. 'The only trouble with my marvellous theory is, why should Murder for Money & Company be interested in bumping off a grotty schoolboy like West?'

'You tell me.' Hackney was sulking. No fewer than four cigarettes now hung from his mouth.

'There's only one person in the world who can tell us,' Crumb muttered. 'And that person is Robin West. We've got to find him!'

Meanwhile, two strange figures were making their way down Bond Street. They were completely wrapped in damp, muddy bandages, and were supporting themselves on crutches. Bond Street is one of the most exclusive, most luxurious streets in the whole of London. Smart little shops sell expensive paintings, expensive clothes, expensive watches . . . anything so long as it's expensive. So the two tramp-like men, who were, of course, Spider and Moss Kito, could not have looked more ridiculous and out of place.

Even so, they had no hesitation in entering one of the smartest clothes shops in the whole street. The shop was called 'MFM Fashions'. Its windows were filled with ties and cravats in bright colours, silk trousers and frilly shirts. It was impossible to say if these clothes were meant for men or for women.

There were only one or two customers in the shop as the two killers entered, and these were too busy looking at themselves in the mirror to notice them. The owner of the shop, a man with mauve hair and rubbery lips, approached them. He didn't seem at all put out by their appearance.

'Can I help you, sweety?' he asked Moss.

'I wish to purchase a striped tie for my uncle,' Moss replied slowly, stressing every word.

'Striped ties are expensive this year,' the owner said, speaking equally carefully.

'Then I'll have two,' Moss said.

'This way, sir.' The man led them into a changing room.

The changing room was like any other changing room in a clothes shop, with four walls, one of which was a full length mirror. On another wall hung a clothes hook, which Spider grabbed and turned round clockwise three times. With a slight click, the mirror swung open to reveal a flight of stairs, going down.

For the 'MFM Fashions' Clothes Boutique was, in fact, nothing less than the front of the secret organization, Murder for Money & Company. The conversation between Moss and the shop-owner (and if you read it again, you'll see it doesn't really make a lot of sense) was an exchange of passwords to allow them entry through the secret door.

The two killers reached the bottom of the staircase where they were stopped by an armed guard in front of a solid metal door.

'Identify yourselves!' he demanded.

'I'm afraid my identity papers got lost in the River Thames,' Moss hissed.

'Then give us this month's special password or die!' the guard ordered.

'Blood and thunder!' stammered Spider.

The guard cocked his pistol and seemed to be about to fire.

'You odious oaf,' growled Moss, kicking Spider on the shin. 'That was last month's. This month's is "broken bones".'

'That's just what you've given me,' wailed Spider, clutching his shin.

The guard relaxed. 'Enter,' he said.

The door slid open to reveal a huge room, seemingly hewn out of solid rock. The air was cold and slightly metallic, filtered by a conditioner that hummed overhead. Neon tubes had been built into the rock, casting a harsh light over the room. One wall was almost completely taken up by a map of the world, with red lights blinking to pin-point the current operations of Murder for Money & Company. The opposite wall was given over to what looked like a giant television screen.

Spider and Moss Kito pressed forward nervously, following an iron walkway down into the middle of the room where a middle-aged lady sat, drinking a cup of tea. She was a very prim and proper lady, rather like a school headmistress. She held her cup with her little finger pointing in the air. She was wearing a neat two-piece suit and she had a pair of spectacles hanging on a cord around her neck.

Her name was Miss Crippen and she was the head of Murder for Money & Company. She was without doubt the most feared woman in the world. Many of her victims had actually shot themselves rather than face up to her and even her closest friends wished that they had never met her.

Seeing Spider and Moss, she put down her cup of tea and scowled.

'You have failed,' she said in a thin, high-pitched voice.

Moss swallowed. Spider's stomach gurgled noisily.

'You have failed twice,' Miss Crippen continued. 'And what is worse, your job was a particularly simple one. My seven-year-old daughter could have managed it better. In fact, I would have given her the job if she wasn't busy polishing off a few foreign ambassadors.'

The television screen suddenly flickered on. It showed a picture of Robin West.

'Robin West. Twelve-years-old. Not even particularly bright . . . at least, if his school report is to be believed.'

A picture of the exploding Mercedes flashed on to the screen.

'And yet you two – supposedly the top employees in my organization and certainly the highest paid – you fluffed it!'

Now the picture changed to show a moving film of the catastrophe on Waterloo Bridge.

'You were almost drowned in your second attempt,' the dreadful woman went on. 'If you fail me again, let me assure you that you will wish you had been!'

The picture went blank.

'Do you have anything to say?'

'I'm very sorry, Miss Crippen,' Spider mumbled.

'Sorry!' There was no emotion in Miss Crippen's voice. There never was. 'Sir Montague Bower was a valued client of mine. I do not wish to disappoint his son. The West boy has made my whole company a laughing stock.'

There was a moment's chilling silence.

'We won't fail a third time,' muttered Moss.

'I hope not, Kito,' Miss Crippen replied. 'For your sake. Have you located the boy yet?'

'No,' Moss whispered.

'We only managed to escape from the Thames by a miracle, Ma'am,' gurgled Spider. 'We haven't had the time . . .'

'I'm not interested in excuses!' The razor-sharp words filled the room. 'I want results. Quickly. This is your last chance, Spider. Otherwise, I shall introduce you to my pets . . .'

Spider broke out in a cold sweat. Miss Crippen's 'pets' were the only things in the world that she loved, and they were deadly scorpions. She had a whole room of them somewhere in the building and knew every one of them by name.

'But I can help you a little,' Miss Crippen continued, picking up her cup of tea once again. 'My agents are everywhere, and we may have a sighting. There is an old woman in Paddington who owns a motor-bike similar to the one which knocked you two fools into the river. We have not yet found out her exact address, but when we do – and it should not be long – we will send it to you. Meanwhile, search the area. But be careful. You mustn't be seen.'

'We'll get the little brat,' Moss said.

'We'll do it,' Spider agreed.

'I promise it,' Moss promised.

'I swear it,' Spider swore.

'You have forty-eight hours,' Miss Crippen said. 'You had better start straight away. And don't make any more mistakes – or else! I want Robin West dead!'

As Spider and Moss left Murder for Money & Company, the boy they were so desperate to find was entering the front door of New Bower House. But even if they had bumped into him then and there, they would have been unable to recognize him. His blond hair was now covered by a black and rather greasy wig. Special heels on his shoes made him several inches taller and a pillow, concealed under his shirt, several inches fatter. He had a large wart on his chin, and he wore thick spectacles and a rather crumpled pin-stripe suit.

Enquiring at the Reception Desk, Robin was directed to an office on the 17th floor where Mr Cringer and Mr Toadwell were conducting interviews for the new lift-operator. As he was five minutes early, he sat in a chair outside the office and waited to be called in.

Presently, a young boy of about his own age and also wearing a crumpled pin-stripe suit, came out and indicated that it would be Robin's turn in a minute.

'You 'ere for the lift job, mate?' he asked cheerily.

'Yes,' Robin said. 'Did you come for it too?'

'Yeah,' the boy replied. 'But I 'aven't got a chance. Them two . . .' he pointed at the office '. . . they're raving loonies if you ask me.'

'What do you mean?' Robin asked.

'Blimey!' the boy said. 'You've got to flamin' hero-worship the boss 'ere. They waffled on abaht 'im as if 'e was some sort of king. I mean to say, I only came 'ere to push lift buttons. But them two . . . Blimey!'

At this point the discussion was ended by a sudden cry of 'Next!' The strange boy winked at Robin and waved his index finger in a small circle beside his head, and with a last 'Blimey!' wandered off down the corridor.

Inside the office, Toadwell and Cringer were seated at a wide table on which various forms and papers had been neatly laid out. They motioned the new applicant to sit down opposite them and then, without even bothering to introduce themselves, began the interview.

First, Toadwell read out a number of questions in a bored voice. As Robin answered them, Cringer quickly wrote on a fresh sheet of paper. They gave Robin the impression that they were doing him a big favour by taking the trouble to see him at all.

'Name?' asked Toadwell.

'Jerry Green,' Robin replied.

'Jerry Green,' Cringer wrote.

'Address?'

'*Dunsailin*, Paddington.'

'Nationality?'

'English.'

'Age?'

'13.'

'Married or single?'

'Single.'

'Education?'

'A bit.'

'None,' Cringer wrote.

'Closest living relative?'

'My mother, Mrs West . . . I mean . . . Green.'

There was a pause while Cringer caught up with the last answer. Then Toadwell, drawing himself up so as to look more important, asked, 'Tell me, Mr Green, why do you want to be a lift-operator?'

Robin had spent the evening before working on his answers, and knew more or less what he had to say. And the boy he had met outside the interview room had also helped him. So, with no hesitation, he replied. 'I want to join the Bower Organization because I think, it's the best company in the world.'

'But why do you want to be a lift-boy?' Toadwell repeated, looking pleased.

'My mother used to operate a lift,' Robin lied. 'And so did my grandmother. Lifts run in the family. I like lifts.'

Toadwell pointed to a picture on the wall behind him. It was a life-size portrait of Frederick Bower, eating an apple pie.

'That is our chairman!' he exclaimed. 'He demands the very highest standards throughout his company. Do you think you could come up to his requirements?'

'Sir,' replied Robin, hoping he wasn't laying it on a bit thick, 'to work for such a great person, such a king of construction is, I know, a great honour for a humble boy like me. I will do my best. I will always press the right buttons. I will keep my uniform clean. I would give my life to make the lift work properly for F. K. Bower Esquire.'

'Such enthusiasm!' cried Toadwell.

'Good, good, good!' crooned Cringer.

'Never have I seen a lift-boy so perfect in his attitude to our illustrious chairman,' Toadwell said. Then, pulling himself together, he turned back to Robin. 'You've got the job. I'm not sure you have the qualifications or the experience, and you're rather tatty, and the wart on your chin is not pleasing to the eye. But if you love our chairman, who is, it must be said, wholly lovable . . .'

'I do,' Robin said, heartily.

'. . . then the job is yours! You start tomorrow at £15.00 a week.'

'The advertisement in the paper said £25.00 a week,' Robin protested.

Toadwell suddenly looked angry. 'That was a misprint,' he explained. '£15.00 a week is more than enough for the honour of working for Mr Bower.'

'Oh yes!' Robin agreed hastily. 'In fact, I was just going to say that I thought £25.00 was a lot too much. Particularly if you're giving away a free portrait of . . . Mr Bower.'

'You're right!' Toadwell said.

'Such intelligence!' Cringer cried.

'Then we'll make it £10.00 a week,' Toadwell decided.

'Hooray!' Robin exclaimed.

Which is how, at £10.00 a week, Robin West became the lift-boy in a firm which, if Toadwell and Cringer only knew it, he actually owned.

9

Up . . . and Down

Robin hated working for Bower Constructors.

The door-man called him 'Sunny-boy'. The receptionist was rude to him. His uniform was far too tight, and no matter how hard he polished them, the buttons refused to shine. Whenever Toadwell and Cringer came into the lift, they would find something to complain about – ash on the carpet, mud on his shoes or simply the time he took finding the right lift buttons to press.

Continually going up and down so fast all day gave Robin a stomach-ache. And the noise of a new building being constructed next door to Bower House gave him a head-ache. The lift was small, with nowhere to sit down, and the whole thing was dreadfully dull.

Robin was seriously thinking of resigning. And he'd only been doing the job for two days! However, he knew that he had to stay. Meg had been most insistent the night before.

'No matter how horrid you think it is, there's always a chance that you'll overhear something useful,' she had said as she attempted to pour medicine down his throat. 'And anyway, at least you'll have a foot in the enemy camp!'

'Maybe if you manage to get Frederick alone in the lift, you'll be able to give him a good thump on the nose,' Mary had added.

But even if that was a nice thought, Frederick hadn't

come anywhere near his lift. And, according to one of the secretaries, he only visited the building very occasionally. Robin had managed to learn that his office was located on the 35th floor of the building and that the doors were triple-locked with very sophisticated alarms directly linked to New Scotland Yard. Furthermore, the corridors were patrolled at regular intervals during the night by armed security guards with ferocious alsations, so the chances of breaking in after the building was closed seemed very remote.

On this day, the second he had worked there, Robin was angry and depressed. The building work going on next door was louder than ever with workmen shouting, hammering and drilling, and the noise seemed to go through his head. This new office-block, an extension to New Bower House, was to be forty-five storeys high, and stood exactly next to the lift-shaft, so Robin suffered from the noise worse than anyone.

Worse still, it had been a particularly busy day. A clerk, who had been sacked by Mr Toadwell for mentioning Frederick's name without slightly bowing his head, had gone from the 17th to the ground floor. He had accidentally taken the tea-lady to the 32nd instead of the 22nd floor, and by the time he had taken her down again, the tea had got cold. So he had to go all the way down to the basement again so she could get some more. Then, one of the more mischievous managing directors had started calling the lift and running away when it arrived.

Up and down, up and down. If you think this all sounds rather dull, you can imagine that for poor Robin who was having to do it all, it was a lot worse.

However, shortly after lunch, when he was beginning

to think that the whole thing was a waste of time, the lift was called down to the ground floor. When the doors slid open, Robin could hardly believe his eyes. There, standing only a few feet away was the one person he most wanted to see: Frederick Kenneth Bower. At last he was face to face with his enemy. For a few seconds the two of them stared right into each other's eyes, though Frederick, of course, did not recognize Robin.

'What are you staring at?' Frederick demanded.

'I'm sorry,' Robin said.

'Please excuse him, Your Wonderfulness,' said Toadwell, who was standing beside Frederick. 'This is a new boy. He hadn't been warned that you were coming.'

'This is an honour!' Robin muttered, assuming a humble look.

'Get out of my way!' Frederick replied as he barged past him into the lift.

He was followed by Toadwell, who was rubbing his hands together anxiously. There was another man with them who was one of the most hideous men that Robin had ever seen. He was more monster than man, and seemed to have only a small brain, to judge from the dull glimmer in his ugly eyes. This, of course, was Gervaise.

'I wouldn't like to meet *him* on a dark night,' Robin thought to himself. To Frederick he said, 'Which floor, sir?'

'35th!' Frederick demanded.

'Uurk!' added Gervaise, positioning himself so that he would be able to stand on Robin's foot as he went out.

The doors shut and the lift began to move upwards.

'To what do we owe the delight of seeing you again so soon?' Toadwell asked, watching the little red numbers above the door as they moved from 1 to 35.

'I've come to see the papers,' Frederick replied.

'The papers?' Toadwell enquired.

'The ones I left in my office. My precious papers, you thick-head,' snapped Frederick. 'And if they're not nice and safe, you and that creep, Cringer, had better look out.'

Toadwell began to perspire. 'Of course they're safe, Your Highness,' he muttered. 'I mean – even if someone did manage to break into your office, and with three alarm systems as well as unusually ferocious guards and dogs patrolling, we all know that's impossible – but just supposing someone did break in, they would never know how to open the safe. I doubt if they'd even realize it was connected to the computer and then they'd have to find the nine-letter password . . .'

'Be quiet, you fool,' shouted Frederick, looking at Robin, who pretended that he hadn't heard.

With a 'ping' the lift arrived at the 35th floor and the doors slid open again. Frederick pushed his way out, followed by Toadwell. Gervaise tried to get Robin's foot, missed, and followed his boss out, growling quietly.

Robin was overjoyed. Frederick kept his papers in a safe in his office. And he could open the safe by keying a nine-letter password into the computer. But what was the word? It could be anything.

He had to find out more and so, without a second thought, he turned the lift off and crept down the corridor, grateful for the fact that the passage was so heavily carpeted that nobody would be able to hear him.

Turning a sharp corner, he just managed to catch sight of Gervaise entering an office before the door slammed shut behind him. One step at a time, Robin stole down the corridor and put his ear against the heavy wooden door. Nobody was saying anything, but now he could hear a dull thumping noise.

Robin bent down and put his eye to the key-hole, wondering what the thudding sound could be. It was soon explained. On Frederick's orders, Gervaise was giving the wretched Toadwell a sound thrashing as a punishment for talking too much in the lift. Robin watched in amazement as the unfortunate manager was thrown around the office by Frederick's brutish assistant.

'All right,' Frederick said, when Gervaise had finished. 'It's time to open the safe.'

'Herro, Mr Fledrick,' said the slightly metallic voice of someone that Robin couldn't see.

'Have you remembered the password?' Toadwell asked, sitting on the carpet and dabbing at his nose.

'Of course I've remembered,' Frederick snapped. 'It's what I love most in the world. How could I forget?'

'And what is that?' Toadwell asked.

'It's . . .'

'What do you think you're doing?'

Robin spun round to find himself in the grip of Cringer who had crept up behind him and who was now staring down at him, a stern look on his face.

'What do you think you're doing?' Cringer

95

demanded again, tightening his grip on Robin's neck. 'Eaves-dropping, were you?'

'No, Mr Cringer, sir,' Robin said. 'I . . . I'm afraid I've lost the lift – and I was wondering if it's in this room.'

'Lost the lift?' Cringer cried. 'Why did you leave it in the first place?'

'To go to the lavatory, sir,' Robin said. 'I was so excited that the chairman, the brilliant Frederick K. Bower, had come into my lift that I just had to go to the loo.'

'Well, this is Mr Bower's office,' Cringer said.

'Is it?' Robin pretended to be astonished. 'Well, well! What a silly mistake! I'm terribly sorry, Mr Cringer. Please don't tell Mr Bower about my ridiculous mistake.'

Cringer, who had no intention of bothering Frederick with what he saw as a small matter anyway, pretended to think about this – just to frighten the new boy – and finally said. 'All right. The lift is back down the corridor, round the corner. But don't let this happen again.'

'No, sir. Thank you, sir. You're a saint, sir,' Robin replied, and then he dashed back down the corridor. Straightening his tie and forcing a weak smile to his pallid face, Cringer then went into Frederick's office.

Robin took the lift back down to the ground floor and found a telephone in order to call Meg. 'Meg!' he said, when she answered. 'I've got wonderful news. Frederick has been into his office, and I think I know where the papers we're looking for are hidden.'

'Robin!' Meg cried, interrupting him. 'Thank goodness you've rung.'

'What's wrong?'

'It's your sister – Mary . . .'

'Is she all right?

'I don't know. She went out by herself while I was preparing the lunch. She said she'd be back in a few minutes, but she's been gone for more than an hour. I'm so stupid! I shouldn't have let her go out by herself. Robin – I think something very nasty may have happened to her . . .!'

Mary gave up trying to escape from the ropes which bound her hands tightly behind her. Her wrists were sore and she ached all over. She couldn't see if her attackers had drawn blood as everything around her was in inky darkness. There was a continuous throbbing in her head and her mouth was dry.

She was in some sort of van. She could tell from the vibrations of the engine and the bumps in the road. The van kept stopping and starting, which suggested that they were still in London rather than on open country roads. At one point she heard someone shouting outside the van and had tried to shout back for help, but the strong strip of tape across her mouth had stopped her.

The smell in the van was horrible. It was the sort of smell that you can't describe to someone unless they've smelt it too. It was a smell of decay; a musty, dark and evil smell. As Mary moved, her legs scraped against some sort of powder that covered the floor of the van – what the powder could be, she had no idea.

Nor did she know for sure who had put her into this horrible predicament. They had been too quick. But Mary thought she could guess who her two kidnappers had been: the so-called 'uncles'. The thought wasn't a very comforting one.

Mary had gone out just before lunch to post a letter to her mother, assuring her that Robin and she were safe and well. Naturally, she hadn't said where they were, as the police would almost certainly read all Mrs West's mail, but she didn't want her mother to worry about them. Meg had fussed a bit about the danger of leaving the boat, but Mary had wanted to catch the one o'clock post and had sworn that she would be all right.

The post-box was a ten-minute walk away, further than she had thought. But she took her time, enjoying a breath of fresh air after being cooped up all morning. She had just posted the letter when she heard a sudden rush of footsteps on the pavement behind her, followed by a squeal of tyres in the road. Before she could even turn round, a hand had grabbed her by the throat, and another hand had clamped itself over her mouth to stop her screaming. They were hairy hands, the hands of the menacing stranger in Pinner.

Almost immediately, the van she had heard had pulled up. Another person got out and together the two had manhandled her into the back. She had tried to fight, but they were too strong. Then she must have hit her head for the next thing she remembered was waking up in pitch darkness with her hands tied behind her. And the van was driving steadily onwards to its unknown destination.

The whole operation had taken less than thirty seconds.

In the front seat of the van, Spider was puzzled. 'Excuse me, boss . . .' he said.

'Yes?' replied Moss, who was driving.

'Why have we kidnapped the girl, Moss?'

'What do you mean, you buffoon?'

'It's just that I'm at a bit of a loss, boss,' explained Spider. 'I thought it was the boy we was after, not his sister.'

'Sometimes I worry about you, Spider,' Moss said. 'You're so witless, you're wonderful.'

'Thanks, boss,' said Spider, who thought this was a compliment.

'Listen!' Moss continued slowly. 'It's simple. Brilliant, I admit, but simple. Through a great stroke of luck we spotted the girl in the street and managed to truss her up like a turkey in the back of the van.'

'Yes, Moss?'

'So she will be the bait with which we entice her horrible brother into our net. When he comes to rescue her, we will be ready.'

'With a hammer?' asked Spider.

'And a mangle,' replied Moss.

'And a carving-knife?'

'And a bone-crusher.'

And the two men were so excited by the thought that they both broke into song:-

'Choppers and mincers
And man-eating lions,
Pokers and pincers,
And smouldering irons,
Manacles, handcuffs and sharp metal rings,
These are a few of our favourite things!

Lying and cheating
And robbing old ladies,

Bashing and beating
And bothering babies,
A bee when it's angry, a wasp when it stings,
These are some more of our favourite things!

When a boy groans,
When a girl cries,
That's the time to smile.
I love to remember my favourite things
For everything seems worthwhile!'

In the back of the van, Mary could hear the noise that Spider and Moss were making and shuddered. For a long time, she hadn't realized that they were actually singing. Moss sounded like a cat in pain and Spider like a sick frog. It was probably just as well that she couldn't make out the words!

The van rumbled along for a bit longer after the assassins had finished their song. At last it stopped. Mary heard a door being pushed open on rusty wheels, the van jerked forward, the doors grated shut, and the engine stopped. A moment later, the door of the van was thrown open and Mary was pulled out.

Spider tore the tape off her mouth as he helped her to her feet. However, he left her hands tied up. The first thing she noticed was that both he and the other man had changed a great deal since she had last seen them in Pinner. They were both a mass of bruises and half-healed cuts. Part of Spider's chin seemed to have been blown off. Moss no longer had any hair or eye-brows. Remembering that it was she who was responsible for this, Mary felt more than a little bit uncomfortable.

'So we meet again,' Moss said, smiling wickedly.

'Allow me to introduce myself. I am Moss Kito and this is my assistant, Spider. You have caused us both a great deal of pain and trouble.'

'Where am I?' Mary demanded, doing her best not to show how frightened she was.

'In a warehouse on the River Thames,' Moss replied. 'Many years ago I used to own a food company which operated from here. A useful side-line, Fungus Foods Limited.'

'Fungus Foods?'

'Yes. It specialized in frozen foods, dried foods, tinned foods, plastic replacement foods and powdered foods; everything, in fact, except for nasty fresh food. This warehouse stored the powdered mashed potato. In fact, the floor above us is stacked with old packets of instant mashed potato.'

'That was the powder in the van,' Mary said.

'How clever of you,' Moss continued. 'Yes. Just add water to the powder and you have a plateful of fluffy mashed potato in a second. It's quick. It's cheap. It's efficient. But unfortunately nobody will buy it as it tastes repulsive.'

Mary looked around her. The ground floor of the warehouse was bare but for a table and two chairs, a few old packing cases and the van in which she had been abducted. The whole place looked about as safe as a card-house in a storm. Everything was rotten. The wooden planks of the floor were warped and damp with clumps of thistles growing out of them in places. The walls – also wooden – were twisted and bent and full of holes which had been hastily patched up with pieces of corrugated iron. Even the ceiling above them seemed to be straining under the weight of the mashed potato upstairs. The beams were almost groaning, curving beneath the wooden platform of the first floor, and threatening to snap at any minute.

'What do you want me for?' she asked.

'A good question!' Moss hissed, his eyes lighting up. 'And let me assure you, my little one, that if you are good and do as you're told, you will come to no harm.'

'But you said I could bash . . .' Spider began.

Moss grabbed his accomplice by the nose. 'Be quiet!' he snarled. Then, smiling at Mary, he added, 'No, no. We won't hurt you, even though you did blow us up. We don't mind, do we, Spider!'

'Doh, Boss!' Spider said, rubbing his swollen nose.

'No. You're going to make a phone call for us,' Moss continued.

'A phone call,' Spider burbled, beginning to giggle again.

'You're going to tell your brother where you are – at the Fungus Food Warehouse on the South Bank of the River Thames, near the National Theatre.'

'Tee hee!' Spider snickered.

'You'll tell him that you're perfectly safe, but that he must come here at exactly seven o'clock this evening to meet you. That you've found something very important. And he must come alone.'

'A trap!' Mary exclaimed.

'Precisely,' Moss said.

'You're a genius, Moss,' Spider cried.

'I won't do it!' Mary shouted.

Moss's face grew dark and angry, and the smile vanished. His two eyes, however, still flickered with a pale light. 'Nobody refuses Moss Kito,' he whispered, his voice as sharp as a cut-throat razor.

'I won't lead Robin into a trap,' Mary repeated, although she was terrified by what might follow.

'I think we'll be able to persuade her,' Moss said to Spider.

'We can drown her!' Spider exclaimed.

'No, you dunderhead,' Moss growled. 'We can't kill her, can we! Because if we do, she won't be able to make the phone call! No. We'll save that treat for her verminous brother. But we *can* hurt her. We can pull her hair!'

'Pull her teeth!'

'Pull her fingers!'

'Pull her legs!'

Moss suddenly spun round to face Mary. 'How would you like to spend half an hour alone with my close friend, the repulsive Spider?' he asked.

Spider giggled in a queer way, stroking Mary's face with one long, hairy finger. 'What fun,' he sniggered. 'Oh what fun!'

'Half an hour with Spider will change your mind.'

'I'll change her face,' Spider hissed.

'But if you were to do as we said – we might not hurt you at all. In fact, we'll let you go,' Moss went on.

'Let her go? We might! We might!' Spider sang.

Mary looked at the two creatures capering around her. Spider had begun to dribble and his eyes were spinning round and round in their sockets, quite out of control. His whole face twitched and his fingers were dancing in bizarre patterns all over his own body. Moss stood silent, gazing at her with a horrid look, his two sharp teeth shining in the gloom. Although he was quieter, he was somehow even madder than Spider and twice as frightening.

She could bear it no longer.

'All right!' she cried. 'I'll do it. I'll do what you want. I'll call Robin and get him here. Only leave me alone . . .!'

10

The Night of the Mashed Potato

'Hello?'

'Mary! Is that you?'

'Robin!'

'Where on earth are you?'

'I hope you haven't been worrying about me.'

'We've been dreadfully worried. What's going on?'

'Listen, Rob. I can't talk much. I'm at the Fungus Food Warehouse on the South Bank of the River Thames, near the National Theatre.'

'What are you doing there?'

'I think I've found something terribly important, Rob. Can you meet me here at seven o'clock this evening?'

'Meg can drive me, but . . .'

'No! You must come alone. I'll explain why when you get here.'

'But Mary . . . !'

'I've got to dash, Rob. It's very important. Be prompt. Seven o'clock. Come by yourself.'

Moss wrenched the phone away from Mary's hand and put it back on the hook. Spider, who had been listening to the conversation through a pair of headphones, removed them and giggled.

'He's coming! Nasty little Robin West is coming!'

'You did well.' Moss folded up the cut-throat razor which only seconds ago had been pressed close to Mary's neck.

'You mustn't hurt him!' Mary cried.

'Oh, mustn't we?' echoed Moss. 'Mustn't we, indeed?'

'We must! We must!' Spider giggled.

'What are you going to do with me?' Mary asked.

'You must wait for your brother to come, since you so kindly called him for us,' replied Moss with a grimace. He looked at the battered watch on his battered wrist. 'It is now a quarter past five. That means he will be here in less than two hours. Take our young friend into the waiting room, Spider!'

Spider grabbed Mary and, before she could protest, lifted her up and roughly carried her further into the warehouse. The whole ground floor was one big room, but now she noticed a small office in the far corner, furthest away from the front door. This was the 'waiting room' which Moss had referred to.

Like the rest of the warehouse, the office was filthy and bare but for a large metal ring, cemented into the floor. It was to this ring that Spider now tied Mary, pulling the ropes around her wrists so tight that they hurt. Then, checking his handiwork, he said, 'Don't run away now!' and laughing merrily at his own joke, turned round and left her.

Run away! Mary could hardly move. She twisted round on her side to try to make herself more comfortable, but any movement only hurt her wrists more. She looked round to take stock of her surroundings. If this had been a play or a television programme, she would have been certain to have found a knife or a piece of broken glass with which to cut her bonds and escape. But, sadly, there was nothing in the office to raise her hopes even for a minute.

106

The room had one window, but it was so heavily barred that even a mouse would have been unable to crawl through. Looking upwards, she noticed a trap-door set in the ceiling. When the warehouse had been in use, this would probably have been the entrance for a ladder to the second floor. But, being so firmly tied down, there was no hope of her being able to reach it – even if she had had a ladder, which she hadn't.

Escape was impossible. Spider hadn't closed the door of the office, and Moss had set up a rickety table nearby. From where they sat, they had a perfect view of both Mary and the front door of the warehouse. They had pulled out a tattered pack of playing cards and were counting out coins, but they weren't so involved that they stopped watching Mary. Every now and then Spider would gaze at her and wink horribly, as if enjoying her unpleasant predicament.

It certainly seemed hopeless. However, despite everything, Mary still had some hope left. Virtually every word of her telephone conversation with Robin had been written out for her by Moss. And with Spider listening in, it had been impossible to warn Robin that she was being forced to lead him into a diabolical trap. But she had still been clever enough to give him a clue. It had been the smallest hint that something was wrong, but it had been the best she was able to do on the spur of the moment. Would Robin have noticed it? Would he understand what was going on?

Sitting in that grim little office, watched over by Spider and Moss, Mary dearly hoped so. She hoped so for both their sakes.

* * *

Robin was sitting in the kitchen of *Dunsailin* with Meg. They were both very puzzled.

'It's not like Mary to dash off like that without telling me first,' he said.

'She said she wanted to get some fresh air,' Meg replied. 'But I'm sure she'd have said if she wasn't going to be back for lunch.'

'It's very peculiar,' Robin agreed.

'Oh dear! I'm too old for all this,' Meg sighed. 'But I'm not sure you ought to go to this warehouse. Not alone, anyway.'

Robin creased his brow. 'There was one thing . . .' he began.

'What was that?'

'On the telephone – she kept on calling me Rob. Not Robin, but Rob.'

'Is that unusual?' Meg asked.

'Yes. In fact it's more than unusual. Mary knows I hate being called Rob. I've got a thing about it. If my name was Anthony, I expect people would call me Tony all the time and I'd hate that just as much. But she kept on calling me Rob – two or three times.'

'Perhaps she was trying to tell you something.'

'That's just it, Meg!' Robin cried. 'If she was being forced to make that telephone call, it might be the only clue she could give me . . .'

'A trap!' Meg exclaimed. 'You're right, Robin. I feel it in my bones. And my bones are never wrong. When you're as old as me, your bones become sensitive.'

'What do you think we ought to do?' Robin asked.

'What can we do? We have to call the police . . .'

Robin shook his head. 'No, Meg. We can't. They'd

never believe us, and by the time they got round to the warehouse it would be way past seven o'clock and who can say what they'd have done to Mary? I've got to go round there myself.'

'But Robin, you don't know what's there. It could be those two men, the ones on Waterloo Bridge . . .'

'She's my sister. I've got to try to rescue her. Listen, Meg. It's half past five now. If I hurry, I can reach the warehouse an hour earlier than they expect me. That way I can take them by surprise. You stay here with Sophocles until half past six exactly, and if you haven't heard from me by then, you can go straight to the police.'

'Can't I come with you? After all, this was all my fault in the first place.'

'No. You've got to stay by the phone.'

Robin and Meg argued for a few more minutes, but whatever Meg said, she couldn't dissuade him and in the end she had to agree that he was right.

'But just you be careful,' she said. 'You've outwitted these men twice. But the third time you may not be so lucky . . . !'

The sun was still shining when Robin arrived at Waterloo Station and set out for the Fungus Food Warehouse. Nonetheless, there was a chilly wind blowing, and Robin found his teeth chattering uncontrollably.

He had no difficulty finding the warehouse which stood out not so much like a sore thumb as a mangled one. From the outside, it looked even more ancient and broken-down than it did from within. In the evening light, it seemed to be coloured grey all over except for patches of red. A battered sign read 'Fungus

Foods' in dripping green paint. The whole building looked as if it was about to topple over into the River Thames, whose murky waters flowed in front of it. It was slanting at an impossible angle. Robin was surprised that anything so delapidated could still exist in twentieth century London.

Once he had made sure that there was nobody on guard, Robin edged up to the front door which had been left slightly ajar. As he moved closer, he was able to make out the voices of two men, somewhere inside.

'You win again, Moss.'

'I always win, Spider.'

'How much do I owe you?'

'Thirty-nine pounds.'

'You're cheating.'

'So are you, you fool. It's just that I cheat better than you.'

Robin peeped through a crack beside the door. Although he could see most of the ground floor of the warehouse, there was no sign of Mary. But in the distance, leaning over an ancient card-table, sat the two deadly assassins who had so nearly blown him up in Pinner.

So it *was* a trap! Robin drew back from the door. There was absolutely no chance of his getting into the warehouse that way without being spotted. Indeed, the two men could see the whole of the ground floor from where they were sitting. What could he do?'

He found the answer round the side of the building. Leading up to the second floor outside the building was a flight of steps, and at the top was an open door. Although half the staircase had been eaten away and the whole thing looked desperately unsafe, it was clearly the only way in. One step at a time, pausing to make sure that each one would hold his weight, Robin began to climb up. Each step creaked noisily, and at one point Robin felt the whole staircase swaying. Fortunately, however, he didn't weigh very much. Had it been Frederick climbing the stairs, for example, the whole thing would have collapsed for sure.

The second floor of the warehouse, although as dirty as the first, was piled high with hundreds of crates. On each crate were stamped the words *Fungus Instant Mashed Potato* in bold red letters, but from the look of them, they had been there so long that the contents must have gone off. Treading very carefully so that his foot-steps wouldn't be heard below, Robin crossed the room, his feet scrunching quietly on a layer of white powder which covered the whole floor.

In the far corner of the room there was a bundle of ropes and beside them, Robin could just glimpse the corner of a trapdoor beneath the dust. He looked at his watch. It was five minutes past six. Meg would call the police in just twenty-five minutes' time.

Kneeling down, Robin gently lifted the trapdoor a few inches, and then pulled it open wider. The first thing he saw was Mary, kneeling right underneath him, her hands tied to a metal ring in the floor. And Mary saw him too. Her eyes widened in surprise as Robin put his finger to his lips to warn her not to cry out. Quickly, she shook her head and then nodded in the direction of Spider and Moss Kito who were still playing cards.

Smiling at Mary to reassure her, Robin closed the trapdoor again. He had to think. Although the two

111

men were engrossed in the card game, Robin couldn't hope to swing down through the trapdoor into the office without their noticing. He would have to create a diversion – something to attract their attention while he rescued his sister.

He looked around him. Except for the crates, there was nothing else that could help him. If only he had thought to bring a box of matches, he might have been able to start a fire. Obviously he couldn't make any noise without revealing that he was there. And time was running out.

Robin was almost at his wit's end when he suddenly saw something which gave him an idea. Against one wall, in the darkest corner, there was a tap. If he turned it on, the water would gradually seep through the floor and finally burst through the ceiling below. The two assassins would assume that a pipe had broken (the tap was rusty enough), and they would have to come upstairs to fix it. And while they were busy, Robin would climb back down and rescue Mary and the two of them would be gone before the assassins knew what was happening.

It seemed to be a fool-proof plan. With great difficulty, Robin managed to turn the tap on and a stream of water began to flood out, landing on the white powder without making too much noise.

He then crossed the room again as quickly as he could, looking for somewhere to conceal himself when the two men came up to see what was wrong. He had only got half-way across when it happened . . .

How could Robin know that several of the floorboards were so mouldy that they were only held together by the moss which covered them? One moment he was running towards a hiding-place, and the next, the floor had simply given way beneath him. With a resounding crash, and a great yell, he fell straight through, through the ceiling of the ground floor and slap bang on to the card-table where Moss was just dealing new hands.

And can you imagine how astonished Moss and Spider were as, in a great ball of white powder and dust, a human missile suddenly landed right on top of the table which immediately collapsed beneath the weight? The two men stood up and gazed at the ceiling where a jagged hole told them what had just happened. In the office, Mary gave a cry of dismay. And then the dust settled, and Moss could see on the floor in front of him, sitting up amid the wreckage of the table, his clothes torn and dirty . . .

'Robin West! How very nice of you to drop in!'

It hadn't been too far to fall, and the card-table had cushioned some of the impact, so Robin was not badly hurt. He felt very bruised, and his mouth was full of disgusting white powder. But worst of all, Robin felt utterly let down (in more ways than one). He had thought he was being so clever, and instead, he had delivered himself into the trap, trussed up like a spring chicken.

'Get the girl,' Moss ordered Spider, who went into the office and released Mary. 'How very delightful it is to see you, Master West,' he continued. 'And an hour early too! Such enthusiasm! And what an unusual way of entering my warehouse! What a shame we won't have a chance to get to know each other a bit better. You really are most amusing. Are you hurt?'

'No,' Robin said.

'What a shame! What a shame! Still, I expect my ghastly friend, Spider, will soon be able to change that.'

Spider now pushed Mary out of the office. She ran over to her brother and knelt down beside him.

'Sorry, Mary,' Robin said, rather weakly.

'It's my fault,' she muttered. 'I should have refused to make you come here.'

'Never mind.' Robin spoke loudly and boldly so that Spider and Moss would hear. 'I rang the police and told them that I was coming here, and they said they'd follow. They'll be here any minute now.'

Moss laughed cruelly. 'Any minute now?' he repeated. 'He says the police are coming.'

'Does he indeed?' crooned Spider.

'Nice try, my little dumpling,' Moss said to Robin. 'But I somehow don't believe you. Would a wanted criminal really be able to get the police to help him?'

'He's fibbing! He's fibbing!' Spider gurgled.

'And we all know what happens to fibbers,' Moss added in an icy tone.

Rubbing the dust off him, Robin got shakily to his feet.

'Up against the wall!' Moss ordered.

Mary helped Robin, who was still rather dizzy, and the two of them walked over and propped themselves up against the wall, a few yards away from Spider and Moss. Mary felt as if she and her brother were standing at the receiving end of an execution squad, an impression made all the more frightening by the appearance of a massive pistol in Moss's bony hand.

'What are we to do with them?' asked Spider, his horrible grin stretched wider than ever.

114

'I thought a little shooting . . .' suggested Moss.

'Too quick!' hissed Spider.

'Then what do you suggest?'

'Ants!' Spider spluttered. 'We'll tie them down and let the ants eat them alive.'

'But there aren't any ants in Waterloo, you chicken-brained Charlie,' growled Moss. 'No. Let's just shoot them and be done with it.'

'No, Moss!' Spider protested in an angry voice. 'I want to have a bit more fun after all they've done to us. I want to push them about. I want to stamp on their toes. I want them to remember us!'

'They're hardly likely to forget us as we're about to bump them off, you dimwit,' returned Moss, growing angrier himself.

Spider and Moss were standing some distance away from Robin and Mary now, and they were gradually getting more and more cross. Both were so excited that they failed to notice a very strange thing. Mary, however, did. She nudged Robin and Robin followed her eyes as she gazed up in the air, above the two squabbling assassins.

The ceiling above Spider and Moss was beginning to bulge. It was growing rounder and rounder every second, as if some enormous weight was pushing on it from above. The whole warehouse was twisted and bent with age, but every second it was becoming more so. And now, even more peculiar, behind the two killers, a steady stream of white, slushy stuff was oozing out of the ceiling and plopping down to the floor below. But Spider and Moss were now arguing so noisily about how they should best deal with Robin and Mary that they heard and saw nothing.

115

It was the water that had done it, Robin suddenly realized. He had turned the tap on upstairs to create a diversion, but the water hadn't had a chance to seep through the ceiling as he had planned. Instead, it had been absorbed by the mashed potato powder.

If you've ever seen your mother preparing instant mash, you'll have noticed that when she pours water on to the white powder, the powder swells up until it becomes several times its own size. This is what was going on upstairs. But instead of one packet of instant mash, there were literally hundreds and hundreds of tons of it. And instead of one small cupful of water, gallons were pouring out every minute. There was no stopping it. Now there was mashed potato plopping down all over the place. Soon there would be so much that the ceiling would be unable to hold it up any longer. Already the wood was creaking loudly and the beams were beginning to splinter and crack.

But the two killers were still shouting at each other, as Mary and Robin watched in awe.

'We'll shoot them!' Moss was yelling.

'Spoil-sport!' Spider cried.

'I'm the boss,' Moss shouted.

'I hate you!' blubbered Spider.

But Moss was quite decided. He had a job to do, and he would do it now. He brought his pistol up and aimed it at Robin. Slowly, his finger found the trigger and began to squeeze . . .

At that exact moment, with a frightful crack, part of the ceiling right above him gave way, and before he could pull the trigger a huge dollop of cold mashed potato landed on his head, blinding him for a moment. Spider looked at Moss in amazement.

116

'What on earth . . .' began Moss.

Spider reached out with a hooked finger and plucked some of the stuff out of his boss's eye. Then he sucked the finger. 'Mashed potato,' he exclaimed.

'Mashed potato?' asked Moss, frowning.

'Mashed potato!' they both screamed, looking up at the ceiling.

'Duck!' Robin shouted to Mary, pulling her aside.

With an ear-shattering crash, the whole ceiling caved in. Spider and Moss were the first to go. Robin just caught sight of Moss, who seemed to be strangling his incompetent friend, and then they were both buried underneath a mountain of mashed potato.

It was everywhere! The whole warehouse began to tremble and then parts of it seemed to explode as the mashed potato forced its way out. Great timbers of wood crashed down, followed by a raging, roaring river of mashed potato.

'Quick!' yelled Robin to Mary above the awful clamour.

The warehouse was being destroyed in seconds. Desperately, the two children sprinted towards the door. Behind them, the mashed potato rose up in huge waves. Pieces of corrugated iron were ripped away from the wall. The potato seemed to have a life of its own as it grew vaster and vaster. Would it never stop?

Robin could feel the cold slime touching the back of his legs. But everything was clear ahead. With one last effort, he threw himself forward, grabbing Mary's hand. The two children just managed to break through the door before the whole warehouse caved in on itself. It was almost as if the potato was actually eating the wood. In seconds, there was nothing left of the place except for the faded sign reading 'Fungus Foods'. Then that, too, was swallowed up by the billowing cloud.

Mary and Robin didn't stop running until they had crossed the river again – across Waterloo Bridge, the same bridge on which they had so nearly been trapped a few days before. Only when they had reached the safety of the opposite bank did they stop and look back. And the sight which met their eyes was almost too incredible to be true. But true it was, and quite, quite terrible.

The mashed potato was still growing. Already it must have measured at least half a mile from one end to the other, and it was as high as St Paul's Cathedral. Whole buildings were being smothered by the vast white mess. It looked rather like some unimaginable creature from outer space.

That evening – which came to be known as The Night of the Mashed Potato – was one of the biggest disasters in the whole of British History. The mash didn't stop growing for another two hours.

Whole buildings vanished. A cargo boat mistook the mash for a thick bank of fog and sailed right into it, never to emerge again. Traffic was stopped for miles around. In the nearby National Theatre, a brand new production had begun its first night. It was *Hamlet*, and they were doing the scene when the ghost appears, and an actor had just said: 'It is a nipping and an eager air,' when suddenly, with a great explosion, one of the walls of the stage burst in, and in seconds the actors had been swept away and the whole stage filled with dirty mashed potato.

As it happens, the audience thought this was meant

118

to be part of the play, and applauded and cheered no end. Indeed, the production was very popular, solely on account of this, and the critics in the newspapers loved it, which everybody agreed made a nice change. But that was the only good thing to come out of the mash disaster.

Nobody would escape from the billowing monster. On platform three of Charing Cross Underground Station, a hundred people ran screaming for their lives when, instead of a train, a great white mess burst out of the tunnel like tootpaste squeezed out of a giant tube. An entire committee of the Greater London Council (who had met to discuss violence in children's books) was literally wiped out. The London Philharmonic Orchestra, playing at the Festival Hall, disappeared completely with a last, despairing blast from the trumpets. Never had Schubert's Unfinished Symphony been quite so unfinished.

Eventually the army was brought in to deal with the situation. After serious talks between generals, lieutenants, captains and corporals, and more talks between ministers, social workers, police and firemen, a solution was finally discovered.

The army was ordered to eat the mashed potato.

Operation 'Spoon and Fork' as it was called took twenty-four hours and by the end of that time, 20,000 soldiers – the whole of the British army – had a terrible stomach-ache.

Robin and Mary's adventure was also over by that time. And just how it all ended must now be revealed.

11
High Adventure

After their narrow escape from the warehouse, Robin and Mary might well have believed that, for a short time anyway, their adventures were at an end. They were both dog-tired, and Mary had begun to shiver all over – a reaction to the shocks she had been through. But when they arrived back at Meg's boat, they discovered that far from ending, their troubles had become worse than ever.

The whole street had been cordoned off by the police. Once again in charge of the operation, Chief Inspector Hercule Crumb was shouting orders and hunting up and down the pavement for clues (quite what he was looking for, nobody knew). There was no sign of Meg, but Mary soon found out from a newspaper-seller, who had witnessed the whole thing, that she had been arrested and taken away for questioning.

What had happened was that at half past six on the dot, there being no word from Robin, Meg had telephoned the police. She had wanted help, but by a stroke of bad luck, had been connected directly to Crumb. Worse still, the line had been a particularly bad one – all crackle and hiss – and Crumb had been able to understand only half of what she had said.

It wasn't really all Crumb's fault. All he could hear on the telephone was something like this: 'Emergency . . . hiss, crackle . . . warehouse on the River Thames . . . buzz, click . . . hello? . . . Fungus Foods . . .

Robin West . . . whirr, tic, toc . . . must come . . . hello? . . . bing!'

In other words, Crumb only grasped a tiny part of the message.

And at exactly the same time as this conversation, reports had begun to flow into New Scotland Yard of a disturbance on the South Bank of the river, of an enormous cloud of white stuff and a warehouse belonging to Fungus Foods which seemed to have exploded.

Crumb had put two and two together and, as usual, he had made five. The old woman who had just rung him, he deduced, was confessing to a terrible crime which she had committed, helped by Robin West. She had blown up the warehouse, presumably to complain about the government's attitude to old age pensioners, the treatment of furry animals, free milk . . . or something else that old ladies tend to complain about.

This was Crumb's deduction. Without further ado, he had called his men together and, in a lightning raid, had surrounded Dunsailin and arrested the occupant. Meg had tried to explain, but he was so convinced that he was dealing with a lunatic, that he had locked her up without listening to a word.

Robin and Mary watched the activities of the police from a safe distance and with heavy hearts. One of the policemen had just found Meg's motorbike, which he recognized as the one which had burst through the barrier on Waterloo Bridge. Everyone was becoming very excited, especially the newspaper journalists and photographers who were all over the place. For it was clear now to everyone (except Crumb) that it had been Meg who had rescued the two children. Another policeman had found Sophocles, who was squeaking most pitifully. But the policeman just roared with laughter until Sophocles was himself charged with impersonating a mouse, put under arrest and carted off to prison.

Robin had gone very pale. His one and only friend, and the only person who knew the truth, had been snatched away. If only he hadn't been captured by Moss Kito, he might have been able to get back in time to stop Meg calling the police. Now he was alone again in a hostile city. It would only be a matter of time before he, too, was caught and locked up, to spend the rest of his life behind bars.

'What are we going to do now?' Mary asked eventually.

'I don't know,' Robin replied. 'Perhaps we ought to give ourselves up.'

'Perhaps you're right.'

Both of them were thoroughly fed up. In fact, their spirits were so low that the thought of a comfortable bed and a hot meal in a little cell sounded most attractive. But neither of them had forgotten that the bed would probably be a hard wooden board. The meal would almost certainly be luke warm porridge. And the little cell would definitely be their home for the next twenty-five years.

Robin was suddenly determined. 'The safe!' he cried.

'What safe?' Mary asked.

'The safe in Frederick's office. I should have told you before . . .'

And he told her all about his experience in the lift at New Bower House; about the safe that was connected to the computer and about the nine-letter word that would open it.

'If only Cringer hadn't come along at that moment, I'd have heard what the password was,' he said. 'But we've got to break in and see what we can do. Once we have the papers, we'll be able to prove that we're innocent, that Meg was right to help us. And then I'll be a millionaire and I'll be able to pay for all the damage that we've caused.'

'But we'll never be able to break into the office,' protested Mary. 'Not if there are guards and electric alarms.

'There is a way,' Robin replied. 'I spotted it the first day I went there.'

'What's the plan?' Mary asked.

'I don't think I'd better tell you,' Robin muttered. 'I have a funny feeling you're not going to like the idea. Not one little bit.'

Two hours later, at nine o'clock, everything was quiet outside New Bower House. A few cars passed the empty building from time to time, disappearing quietly into the darkness. A rat scurried across the pavement to rummage in an overflowing dustbin. A slight breeze blew a tattered sheet from an old newspaper along the deserted pavement.

Then the front door of New Bower House opened and two uniformed men stepped out. Beside them, on a long metal leash, a huge Alsatian with no tail padded silently along. One of the men was smoking a cigarette. The other carried a torch which he now turned on, sweeping the road with a powerful beam of light.

The two men were security guards. The Alsatian was a security dog. They were just beginning their regular patrol round the premises to check for

123

intruders. They both wore leather belts, from which hung heavy wooden clubs.

One of these guards had been a professional wrestler until he had tied his opponent into such a difficult knot that it had taken three doctors a month to undo him. The other guard had been a senior officer in the army, although he rarely talked about it. It had been the Russian army. As for the Alsatian, it had once won the top prize at the Crufts Dog Show . . . but only by eating all the other competitors. The three were very happily employed by Bower Constructors.

They continued their patrol, slowly and surely, but there was nobody in sight. However, when they reached the building site next to New Bower House, the dog suddenly stopped. Its ears pricked up and it uttered a low growl.

'What is it, Fang?' asked one of the guards.

Fang growled more loudly.

'Do you see anyone?' the other guard asked.

'No. Not a soul.'

'Me neither.'

However, Fang continued to mutter in its doggish way, its hackles rising. Normally, the two guards would have ignored its performance, for the dog was so stupid that once it had even bitten off its own tail. But only the day before they had received a note from the chairman, Frederick K. Bower himself. The note had ordered them to keep a special eye out for 'a small boy with fair hair, aged about twelve.'

But neither a small boy nor anybody else was in sight. The guards tramped all round the building site. They looked in the pile of rubble beneath the crane which towered above them. They examined the pits and the trenches. They looked behind huts and underneath the lorries. But although Fang barked, whined and frothed at the mouth, there was nothing.

They did not, however, think to look approximately 100 metres up in the air.

Robin was gazing at the two guards. He was as still as a statue, scarcely breathing in case they heard him. And a little way above him, Mary was hanging on for dear life, her face pale and her eyes squeezed tightly shut.

This was Robin's way into Frederick's office – the crane. Like most building sites, the one next to New Bower House had its own crane to lift bricks and things up and down on to the new building. It was 150 metres high. At the top of the crane, some 6 metres above the control box, a long iron arm stretched out into open space, stopping just short of New Bower House. And by sheer good luck, the very end of the arm was only a metre away from Frederick's window. And the window was open. He never bothered to lock it as it was, after all, more than 100 metres above the ground.

The arm was about 60 metres long. Robin had quite simply decided to climb up the crane, somehow make his way along the arm, jump the last metre on to the window sill and then climb into Frederick's office to crack the safe.

It's hard to believe that a few weeks before, he would have hesitated to climb even a small tree, he had such a poor head for heights. But it is a general truth (and several generals will tell you so) that if events demand them, you will be able to find all sorts

125

of qualities hidden in yourself. And as far as Robin could see, there was no other way.

Actually, it had been quite easy up to the point when the two security guards appeared. Every crane has a ladder and although it would be extremely unwise to try it, it was really no more difficult to climb than any other ladder, although it was more tiring because it was so much longer. But when Robin heard the scrunch of the guard's footsteps on the gravel and the growling of the dog, he made a bad mistake. He had looked down.

From where he was, just above the control box, the two guards looked no bigger than matchsticks. The ground seemed to be miles and miles away. He imagined himself falling from his perch, and for a dreadful moment he felt sick and dizzy and his fingers became so weak that it took a great effort to hold on to the ladder. His heart seemed to shrink. His stomach felt like a spin-drier. His mouth became as dry as the Sahara Desert.

But as soon as the two guards had left, he let out a great gasp of breath and forced himself to start climbing again. Mary had already reached the top and was waiting for him, doing her best not to look down. Rung by rung, Robin pressed on. He knew that if he lost his nerve now, he would be lost altogether. It's just a ladder, he told himself, blotting out of his mind the distance between him and the ground beneath.

At last, the sweat pouring from his face, he pulled himself over the top and on to a small platform where Mary was sitting. She was panting with exertion and her face was as white as a sheep (sheets these days being generally coloured).

'We're never going to do it,' she gasped. 'Not in a hundred years.'

'It'll be easy,' Robin said.

This was about a hundred miles from the truth. The long arm of the crane, unlike the ladder, had no regular hand or foot-holds. Steel girders criss-crossed over the steel cable which ran the whole length of the arm, but there were yawning gaps between each one. There was a hand-rail, but it had been built for an adult quite a bit taller than Mary or Robin. And to make matters worse, what had seemed a gentle breeze at ground level, was more like a hurricane at 100 metres. The arm of the crane was swaying in the wind, and icy blasts threatened to blow them out into space to a fast but fearful death.

They set off.

'Don't look down,' Mary warned Robin. 'Pretend you're crossing a river on stepping-stones.'

'In a force nine gale?' Robin asked, gritting his teeth.

One pace at a time, they moved across the arm, straining to keep their balance against the wind. Mary had gone first, closely followed by her brother. She kept her eyes in front of her, concentrating on the distance between each girder. To take too long or too short a step would be disastrous. The great wall of New Bower House moved gradually nearer.

Then Mary slipped.

She had been going too quickly and had missed her footing. For a ghastly second the world spun around her as she fell, and a single shriek escaped from her lips.

But she didn't fall. For Robin, who had been right

behind her, had just managed to grab hold of her skirt, and as she fell, he had given her one hard pull. So instead of falling right through the gap between the girders, she managed to seize the girder on which she had been standing. Although he was nearly pulled off balance by her weight, Robin managed to let go of her skirt and at the same time take her arm. Then, digging his heels in for support, he pulled his sister back up and helped her to her feet.

The good angels must have been on their side, for twenty minutes later they reached the end of the arm. At this point, exactly above the great steel hook that swung in the wind below them, there was another small platform where they could pause and regain their breath.

'It's funny,' Mary gasped. 'A workman could do what we've just done in less than a minute.'

'Great,' Robin said. 'Perhaps we can get a job as crane-repairers when we grow up. Or maybe we could do it part-time in the holidays.'

'I expect you have to be in a union,' Mary replied.

Ten minutes later, when they had rested themselves enough, Robin and Mary took the final step in their ordeal. In fact, it was more of a jump than a step. There was a gap of one metre between the end of the crane and the window-sill outside Frederick's office. The distance may not have been great. The distance to fall if they missed certainly was.

Mary went first. Again, she didn't look down but, taking a deep breath, plunged out into space. She landed perfectly, and a few seconds later had climbed into the safety of Frederick's office.

Robin was less fortunate. He too landed precisely

on the window-sill, but, perhaps because he weighed more than his sister, part of the concrete beneath his feet gave way as he landed. If he hadn't managed to grab hold of the window at the same time, he would have fallen to his death. Even so, he had to hang there terrified as the concrete fragments clattered to the ground. He waited a full minute, but to his overwhelming relief, nobody came to investigate the sound. Then, with his last ounce of strength, he pulled himself up and climbed through the window, to collapse in a grateful heap on the carpet inside the office.

'What kept you?' Mary panted.

'I just thought I'd hang about a bit outside,' Robin said.

He wanted to rest, but there was work to be done. Standing up again, he crossed the room and pulled a rug to cover the crack under the door. Then he pulled all the curtains shut and, having made sure that it wouldn't be seen, turned the light on.

With the light came an enormous feeling of warmth and security. Mary had thrown herself into a chair and seemed to be asleep. Robin, too, stood silent for a moment. He thought of Spider and Moss, of poisoned chocolates and exploding cars. He remembered Mcg and Sophocles and the canal-boat in the middle of a row of houses. He imagined that his mother or Mr Sylvester or some of his schoolfriends had been in the Fungus Foods warehouse or had watched him breaking into the office. A strange smile came over his tired face.

'Mary?' he said.

'Mmmmmm?'

'I'll tell you something . . .'

129

'What?'

'I bet you all the tea in China that nobody is every going to believe all this. Not in a hundred years!'

Exit Frederick K. Bower

'It's just a computer like any other,' Robin said.

'I don't think so,' Mary muttered.

'Nor do I,' the computer agreed.

Robin and Mary looked at each other in astonishment, then back at the computer which winked at them cheerfully. Even without its Japanese voice, it certainly was a very strange machine. It was shaped rather like a grand piano, with computer keys instead of piano keys and a TV monitor where the music-stand should have been. Sitting down, facing the screen, Robin could almost imagine himself giving a concert recital.

It was just as well that the computer could talk. Although both Robin and Mary had learnt a bit about computers at school, it would have taken them weeks to work out the various dials and buttons on the control board. And working out how to programme the machine to open Frederick's safe would have taken them the rest of their lives.

Now Robin cleared his throat and – feeling rather awkward to be talking to a machine – said: 'Excuse me . . . er . . . did you say something?'

'Yes. I am erictronic talking computer, made in Tokyo.'

'Eric Tronic?' Mary asked.

'I think it means electronic,' Robin said. He turned

back to the computer. 'Can you open the safe?' he enquired.

The TV monitor flickered. The tapes turned and the lights flashed. 'Safe-opening sequence plogrammed. Prease pless Start key to begin sequence.'

Robin ran his eye across the keyboard. There was a large, red button labelled, simply, 'START'. He pressed it. There was a pause, then the figure 5:00 appeared on the screen, almost immediately changing to 4:59, 4:58 and so on as it began a five-minute count-down.

'There you are,' Robin said. 'I told you there was nothing to it.'

Mary was not so sure. 'What do the figures mean?' she asked.

'It probably takes five minutes to open the safe,' Robin said.

Twenty seconds had passed.

'Hello? Eric?' Mary leant across and addressed the computer again. 'Why are you telling us the time?'

'You now have four minutes, thirty-one seconds to key in secret password,' the computer told her.

'But we don't know the password.'

'Then in four minutes, twenty-six seconds, erictronic talking computer will commit hari-kiri.'

'You mean . . . you'll self-destruct?' Robin asked.

'Yes. Huge bang. Entire building utterry destroyed. With people in too.'

The smile was fading rapidly from Robin's face.

'Try something!' Mary exclaimed.

'If incollect word fed in, exprosion will be immediate,' the computer said. 'You now have four minutes and four seconds to key in password.'

'Forget it!' Robin cried. 'Turn yourself off. Go to sleep. Pretend I never asked . . .'

'Impossible!' The computer sounded almost sad. 'Sequence started. Cannot stop. Three minutes and fifty seconds to go . . .'

There was something else that Robin and Mary didn't know about Frederick's computer. It had one extra security device built into it. If you pressed the Start button twice, it would function normally. But if you pressed it once – as Robin had – then secret alarms would be triggered in both Frederick's home in Hampstead and in New Scotland Yard.

It was nine o'clock exactly and Frederick was soaping himself in his king-size bath. This bath was so big that you needed a ladder to get out of it and instead of a plastic duck, a real one had made its nest between the taps. Frederick, who was wearing a pink bath-cap to stop his hair getting wet, was completely surrounded by bubbles. A plate of marshmallows stood nearby.

He was just about to pop another into his mouth when a red light above the wash basin started to blink on and off.

'What . . . ?' Frederick began, accidentally swallowing a mouthful of hot water. 'Groogh!' He spat it out again. Then, knocking the marshmallows into the bath (where they were immediately gobbled up by the duck) he climbed out as fast as he could and ran, stark naked, into the corridor.

'Gervaise!' he shouted, soap and water dripping on to the carpet.

'Uuurk?' asked Gervaise, appearing from the television room.

'Get the Rolls!' Frederick snapped. 'Now!'

And without even pausing to think where his master wanted to go, why he wanted to go there, and what he was going to do with no clothes on, Gervaise sped to the garage.

At the same time, Hercule Crumb was tucking into a late supper in his office at New Scotland Yard. Bangers and mash were on the menu that night, but in view of what had taken place a few hours before, Crumb had decided to do without the mash. Hackney, who rarely ate, was sitting opposite him, smoking a cigarette.

'This woman with the motorbike,' Crumb was saying as he jabbed his fork into a sausage. 'This . . . Meg. Do you believe her story?'

Hackney thought for a while. 'Yes, sir,' he said at last, puffing out smoke. 'I mean, it's so unlikely, it's got to be true.'

Crumb held up the sausage on the end of his fork. 'So Frederick Bower is really Robin West and Robin West is really Frederick Bower. It's incredible, Acne. If only we had proof . . .'

At that moment, a bell set in the wall just behind Crumb's head began to ring. Crumb spun round, the sausage flying off his fork to disappear behind a filing cabinet.

'What's that?' he cried.

'It's the alarm in New Bower House,' Hackney said. 'Someone must be trying to break in.'

'Who?'

'It could be Robin West.'

'Come on, then!'

So even as Robin and Mary were talking to the

134

computer, two cars were tearing through the streets of London, both of them making for New Bower House.

The TV screen on the computer showed 2:13. There were just over two minutes left.

'Let's get out of here!' Mary cried.

'We haven't got time!' Robin was tearing at his hair. 'It'll blow up before we can get anywhere. We've just got to think . . .'

'Think about what? Our funerals?'

'No. The password. Come on, Mary. We know it's a nine-letter word. And we know it's the thing that Frederick loves more than anything else in the world. We must be able to work it out.'

'But we can't even make one mistake,' Mary exclaimed.

'This wretched computer . . .' Robin groaned.

'Letched?' the computer said.

The figures on the screen changed again. 2:00, 1:59, 1:58 . . .'

Robin forced himself to concentrate. In front of him, the computer was flashing and blinking, its tapes turning. Now it had begun to hum quietly to itself, a brief extract from the Funeral March before it blew itself, and the children, to smithereens.

'A nine-letter word . . .' Robin said.

'How about . . . explosion?' Mary suggested.

'No. Frederick doesn't love explosions.'

'He's going to love this one.'

Robin was running words through his head, counting the letters. It was so difficult without a pen and a sheet of paper and there was so little time. What did he know about Frederick? What did Frederick love most in the world?

'What about . . . investment?' Mary said.

Robin shook his head. 'It's got to many letters.'

'Then . . . chocolate. Frederick loves chocolate.'

Quickly, Robin counted the letters. There were nine of them. Could the password be 'chocolate'?

'He couldn't forget it,' he muttered to himself. 'That was the point. It was a word he couldn't forget.' A picture of the statue of Frederick outside New Bower House flashed into his mind. 'Lollipops!' he cried.

'Lollipops?' Mary repeated.

'He's holding a lollipop in the statue. He paid me in lollipops when I was a lift-boy. Frederick loves lollipops.'

'Then try it . . .'

The numbers on the screen seemed to be changing faster than ever. 1:02, 1:01, 1:00, 0:59 . . . There was less than a minute to go.

Robin turned back to the keyboard. He could feel that sweat running down the back of his neck and his hair was sticking to his forehead. He stretched out his index finger and tried to hold it over the L-key, but his hand was shaking so much that he was frightened he would miss.

'Lollipops,' he whispered.

It made sense. It had nine letters. It was something Frederick loved. But if it was wrong . . .

0:17, 0:16, 0:15 . . .

He forced his hand down.

'Wait a minute!' Mary shouted.

She brushed past Robin and paused in front of the keyboard.

136

'Mary . . .?' Robin began.

'No.' Mary's eyes were bright with excitement. 'A nine-letter word. Something Frederick loves. Something he couldn't forget . . .'

'Yes, but . . .'

'I've got it!'

And before Robin could stop her, she had tapped in a nine-letter word.

Nothing happened.

0:5, 0:4, 0:3 . . .

Robin reached across and stabbed at the ENTER key.

0:2 . . .

There was a loud buzzing. Behind them, the door of the safe swung open.

Neither of them spoke.

'Clipes, that was crose!' the computer said.

Weakly, Robin got to his feet and embraced his sister. 'Mary,' he sighed. 'You're a genius.' Then a second thought came. 'I didn't even see the word you typed in,' he said. 'How did you know that "lollipops" was wrong?'

Mary was still shaking all over from the tension.

'It was the letter Frederick sent us with the box of chocolates,' she explained. 'We don't know much about Frederick, but we do know that he's a rotten speller. He wouldn't have been able to spell "lollipops" to save his life.'

'Well, you've just saved ours,' Robin said. 'So what was the word?'

Mary laughed. 'It was quite easy after I'd thought of that,' she said. 'It wasn't just a word he'd remember,

137

but a word he'd remember how to spell. The password was his own name: FREDERICK.'

'And that's what Frederick loves more than anything in the world,' Robin added.

'Enter Frederick K. Bower,' Mary said.

Now it was Robin's turn to laugh. 'Let's look in the safe,' he said. 'And all I can say is, after all the trouble we've been to, the birth certificate had better be there!'

It was. The first thing that Robin pulled out was the photograph of himself and the three letters that Meg had once sent Sir Montague Bower. Next there were a couple of newspaper clippings concerning the birth of Sir Montague's son and heir. Both of these stories contained photographs of the new baby – but, of course, it was a photograph of Robin rather than of Frederick, for they had been taken before the exchange had been made.

But it was the last piece of paper in the safe that was the one that Robin and Mary were looking for. It was a copy of Robin's birth certificate, and it described the birthmark that Frederick now carried.

'That's all the proof we need,' Robin said.

'We've found it!' Mary cried.

'Put your hands up!' Frederick shouted.

Both of them spun round. There, at the door, a heavy gun in his fleshy hand, stood (now fully dressed) Frederick Bower, and next to him, a brutal smile on his face, was Gervaise.

Robin and Mary had been so absorbed in the contents of the safe that they hadn't heard the door open. Now it was too late. Frederick kicked it shut behind him and locked it. They were trapped.

'Don't move,' Frederick commanded, threatening

them with his gun. Grabbing the papers from Robin, he threw them in the safe and closed it.

Robin brought his hands down as Frederick went and sat behind the desk. He was determined to show Frederick that he wasn't afraid of him, even if it was the last thing he did – which, from the looks of things, it very well might be.

'What are you doing in my office?' Frederick asked, smiling unpleasantly.

'It's my office,' Robin replied, defiantly.

'How did you know the papers were here?' Frederick demanded.

'It was me in the lift,' Robin explained. 'I was disguised as a lift-boy and I overheard Mr Toadwell.'

'Bother that Toadwell!' Frederick yelled. 'I always knew that I should have sacked him. And that no-good Cringer. I hate them both. Gervaise! Remember to break every bone in their bodies when you next see them. And in their mothers' bodies. I want them all minced.'

'Uuuurk!' Gervaise said.

Mary said nothing. She could not believe her eyes. She had never imagined that the richest boy in the world would behave in such a sulky, spoilt manner.

'I suppose you think you're clever,' Frederick whined.

'Well, since you mention it . . .' Robin began.

'Well, you're not. You're not at all clever. You're the most stupid person I've ever met.'

'No he isn't,' Mary protested, rising to the defence of her brother. 'He's outwitted all your murderers for a start. And he's found the papers.'

'The papers!' Frederick repeated, waving the gun in

Mary's direction. 'Oh yes! He may have found the papers, but a fat lot of good they're going to do him because before we leave here I'm going to open the safe again and burn them to a cinder. And you two will be dead anyway, so there!'

'Can't we be friends?' Robin enquired with his most engaging smile.

'Friends!' Frederick exploded. 'I don't have any friends! And even if I did, you wouldn't be one of them.'

Robin thought about punching Frederick on the nose. He certainly wasn't going to let himself be shot without a fight, not after coming so far. But unfortunately, the beast-like Gervaise was standing too near him. One move, and those great, muscular arms would be around him. He would be squeezed to pulp before he could so much as blink. There seemed to be nothing he could do.

'You can't kill us!' Mary said.

'Why not?' Frederick demanded. 'I can do anything I want to.'

'If you kill us, the police will start asking awkward questions,' she replied.

'The police do what I tell them!' Frederick declared. 'And anyway, who are you to talk? Nasty little criminals! If I do kill you, and I most certainly shall, they'll probably give me a medal.'

He moved across the office and pulled back the curtain which hung over the open window. 'How did you get in here?' he asked Robin.

'Along the crane,' Robin told him.

'I don't believe you.'

'It's true.'

For a moment, Frederick couldn't help admiring Robin. He had never been able to climb anything; just one of a hundred sports that he was totally unsuited for. But admiring him only made Frederick more angry. That Robin should be able to do something that he, the richest boy in the world, couldn't, was almost too much to bear.

His face broke into an ugly smirk. He pulled the window wide open. 'Well,' he said, 'if you came in by the window, you can jolly well leave by the window too! Gervaise!'

Gervaise lumbered forward obediently and laid a huge hand on each of the children's shoulders.

'When the police come,' Frederick explained, 'we'll tell them that you tried to escape along the crane and fell off. Then I'll be left alone in peace and quiet to enjoy my fabulous wealth and you'll both be squashed tomatoes.'

'You can't do this!' Robin cried.

'Oh shut up!' Frederick scowled. 'You two have been nothing but trouble. I wish I'd left you alone in the first place. Then none of this would have happened.'

Frederick stood facing his two helpless victims, his back to the open window. 'Bring them over here and throw them out,' he ordered. 'I never want to see them again. Never.'

Although Robin and Mary struggled and squirmed, they were no match for the gigantic chauffeur who pulled them inch by inch towards the open window. To have come so far, with the proof of all that had taken place twelve years ago so near them, was too much for Mary.

141

'Please, Frederick!' she pleaded.

Frederick ignored her.

'Forget it, Mary,' Robin cried, twisting in Gervaise's grip. 'He's insane. And anyway, his name isn't Frederick. That's my name. He was christened Robin Sponge.'

The name seemed to have an electrifying effect on Frederick. He stepped back a pace, his face a mask of hatred. 'Don't call me that!' he screamed. 'Don't ever call me that.'

But it was too late.

As soon as Robin had uttered the words 'Robin Sponge,' Gervaise had dropped him and his sister and had stopped dead in his tracks. His mouth fell open to reveal a line of grey, broken teeth. He brought a massive paw up to his forehead and scratched his bald skull. A wobbly smile appeared on his lips. One great tear trickled out of the corner of his eye and fell with a 'plop' on to the carpet.

For Gervaise's full name was Gervaise Sponge. Twelve years ago, he had been the drunken taxi-driver who had been married to Ruby Sponge. He had been the father of a boy called Robin who, he thought, had been adopted after his wife had emigrated to Australia. After that, he had found himself a job and had ended up as a chauffeur and bodyguard to the richest boy in the world. To Frederick Bower. But Frederick was really Robin Sponge. Frederick was his son!

'My baby!' he crooned.

'Gervaise!' Frederick yelled. 'Throw those two creeps out of the window!'

'My little boy!' Gervaise sighed. 'My Robin!'

He rushed forward to embrace Frederick.

142

Frederick panicked. For a moment he was faced with the sight of the weeping giant rushing towards him. He picked up his pistol and fired.

The bullet hit Gervaise in the chest.

But still he came on, tears streaming down his face, the strange little smile flickering on his lips.

Frederick fired again.

But then Gervaise had reached him and was smothering the fat boy with his enormous arms. 'My Robin!' he warbled.

And then, dizzy because of the two bullets which had been fired into him, he somehow tripped and toppled forward. With a ghastly scream, Frederick was forced backwards over the sill of the window, which was right behind him. Together, the father and his long-lost-son vanished into the night.

And at the same moment, the door was forced in with a great crash of splintering wood and Chief Inspector Hercule Crumb somersaulted into the office, hitting his head on the desk. Behind him, Hackney and five other policemen charged into the room, guns drawn and ready.

Crumb sat up and looked around him. 'Are you Robin West?' he asked.

'I am . . . sort of,' Robin replied.

'The original Robin West just fell out of the window,' Mary said.

'Except that he was really Robin Sponge,' Robin added.

'Will somebody please tell me what's going on?' Crumb moaned.

'Help!' Frederick cried.

Everyone rushed to the window and looked out.

You may remember that the end of the crane was only a metre away from Frederick's open window, and that beneath this swung a heavy, iron hook. Gervaise and Frederick had fallen about thirty metres and the two of them would have hit the pavement with a nasty 'splat' in about two and a half seconds' time had not Gervaise's belt caught on to this hook. So they had ended up suspended in the air, swaying gently in the breeze, with Gervaise still embracing Frederick and smothering him with kisses.

'Crumbs!' said Crumb. 'Come on men!'

And quite forgetting about Robin and Mary, Crumb and the other policemen rushed out of the room to rescue Frederick.

Robin opened the safe again and took out the precious papers. 'Well, that would seem to be that,' he said.

'That's that,' Mary agreed.

Robin put his hand round his sister's shoulder. He was hungry and tired and at that moment all he felt like was a hot meal, a hot bath and a warm bed.

'Let's go home,' he said.

And they did.